<u>THE</u> <u>OLD</u> <u>RUSSIAN</u> <u>SCIENTIST</u> <u>WAS</u> <u>THE</u> <u>MOST</u> <u>WANTED</u> <u>MAN</u>
<u>BETWEEN</u> <u>MOSCOW</u> <u>AND</u> <u>MARRAKESH</u>—

RAFEI, small-time Lebanese racketeer, wanted
      him for a big-time ransom in American
      dollars.

JANOS KORLA, Yugoslav dealer in drugs,
      prostitution, and international
      blackmail, wanted him as an insurance
      policy on his fast-growing crime empire.

THE CHINESE wanted him for his specialty . . .
      a bombardment system that would bring the
      Russians to their knees!

THE KGB wanted him dead—immediately!

NICK CARTER WAS CAUGHT IN THE FOUR-WAY CROSSFIRE.
HE HAD TO GET SALOBIN OUT ALIVE—BEFORE AN
"ACCIDENT" SENT THE DEFECTOR'S SECRET
INFORMATION TO AN UNMARKED GRAVE!

THE TURNCOAT

Nick Carter

A UNIVERSAL BOOK
published by
the Paperback Division of
W. H. ALLEN & Co. Ltd

A Universal Book
Published in 1978
by the Paperback Division of
W. H. ALLEN & Co. Ltd
A Howard and Wyndham Company
44 Hill Street, London W1X 8LB

Originally published in America by
Universal-Award House, Inc., 1976

Printed in Great Britain by
Hazell Watson & Viney Ltd, Aylesbury, Bucks

ISBN 0 426 18518 8

The exciting, cosmopolitan atmosphere of Beirut has, of course,
been drastically changed by the events of the civil war. Nick's
adventures in Lebanon portray that city as it once was.

Dedicated to The Men of the
Secret Services of the
United States of America

THE TURNCOAT

CHAPTER 1

It was a little past ten when I pushed my way into the crowded Club Salah, a smoke-filled bar in Beirut's native quarter.

There was no room up front, but after glancing around, I spotted an empty booth in the rear alongside the dime-sized dance floor. When I eased myself in and settled back against the stained leather seat, a waiter scooted my way. He was about as tall as a barstool, with bright eyes and a matching smile.

He gave me a quick up-and-down look and nodded approvingly. *"Kayf halik,"* he whispered confidentially. *"Inglizi?"*

I shook my head. *"Amricanee."*

"Aha, *Amricanee.* You see, I speak the English good. I have many cousin in America. One is name of Ahmed. He live Detroit. You know Ahmed, maybe?"

When I told him I wasn't from Detroit, and there was no way I'd know his cousin, he shrugged it off and flicked his soggy napkin toward the three girls at the end of the bar. Two were typical Lebanese—dark haired and plumpish—but the third girl was a stunning redhead, shapely, and in her early twenties. When she noticed us looking her way, she smiled brightly and raised her glass.

The little waiter's elbow nudged my arm. "Her name Hananna. Very friendly girl. She speak the English, too. You like, I bring."

I was tempted, but I shook my head. "Look," I said. "I'd appreciate it if you'd do me a favor. I'm here to see a man named Rafai. Do you know him?"

"Rafai?" The waiter's eyes popped slightly and his smile vanished. "I know Rafai. But why you want to see?"

"Just tell him the *Amricanee* is here."

He thought it over briefly, nodded, and took off like a flushed rabbit. In about three minutes he was back, carrying a shot glass on a small, battered tray.

"I speak to someone," he whispered as he set the glass down. "He say Rafai not here now. But you wait, have drink. When Rafai come, I bring. Ho-kay?"

He was smiling again, so I smiled back and slipped a folded pound note into his hand. When he scampered off, I sniffed at the drink. It was brandy, but by no means first rate; and I make it a rule never to drink anything in places like the Club Salah unless I see it poured. I pushed the glass aside, got out a cigarette and lit up. Suddenly I felt pretty bushed.

My day had begun in an unexpected rush a few minutes before eight that morning when the phone in my Washington hotel room jolted me awake. It was Della Stokes, Hawk's very efficient secretary.

"Sorry to break in on you, Nick," she said, "but *he* wants to see you."

"But I'm supposed to be on vacation," I muttered sleepily.

"Not anymore," she replied crisply. "See you soon."

The one thing you don't do with Hawk is play it

cute. When the old man gives an order, you jump. It took less than ten minutes to pull on some clothes, brush my teeth and shave. When I hit the street a light rain was falling, but the doorman's whistle brought a cab to a fishtail halt. The drizzle had made D.C.'s morning traffic worse than usual, and by the time the cabbie dropped me on the west side of Dupont Circle, another twenty-five minutes had dragged by.

I lost another three minutes taking the elevator up, and when I strode through AXE's outer office Delia glanced up from her chattering IBM.

I nodded toward Hawk's closed door. "How's the climate?"

She smiled sweetly and gave me the thumbs-down gesture. Bracing my shoulders, I turned the knob and went in.

"About time," Hawk growled.

I started to say something about the weather and the traffic, but he shook his head impatiently. "Never mind," he interrupted. "How's your Arabic, Nick?"

That was vintage Hawk. Always to the point. Never wasting words in small talk if he could help it.

"It's been a while, sir," I replied. "I suppose I could use some brushing up."

He grunted, reached inside his desk's top drawer and came up with one of his foul cigars. Clamping it between his lips, he lit up and slowly exhaled a cloud of eye-smarting grey smoke. "Does the name Gregor Salobin ring a bell?"

It rang quite a few.

"He's Russian, of course," I replied promptly. "Probably one of their best missile authorities. I believe he perfected the Soviet's Fractional Orbital Bombardment System, and it's talked around that he's had a hand in planning the Tallinn Defense network. I also think he served as a combat engineer in World War II, received the Lenin medal for bravery and lost his left eye during the battle of Stalingrad. I guess he'd be in his late fifties or early sixties now—wouldn't he?"

If Hawk was impressed he didn't show it.

"Good to see that you keep up with our files, N3," he responded dryly. "But there are some facts about Salobin you don't know." Dipping back inside the desk drawer, he produced a thick folder and tossed it my way. "Find a quiet corner and read this through. When you've finished, come back and we'll talk about it."

The material took more than an hour to digest, but it made fascinating reading. I was right about Salobin's missile expertise, but the real kicker came when I read that Salobin had been passing on vital missile data to U.S. Intelligence for close to three years.

According to the ITG-4 fact sheets, prepared by Salobin's American controller in Moscow, the Russian wasn't in it for the money. It was an ideological thing, brought on by Salobin's growing disenchantment with his Kremlin bosses. Repeatedly, the fact sheets kept pointing out how Salobin expressed harsh criticism of his government's harassment policy toward scientists or any other Russian citizen who disagreed even slightly with their leaders.

When I had finished reading the material I took another look at the small snapshot of Salobin that was part of the dossier. It showed him standing in front of a small country house, probably his *dacha* in a Moscow suburb. I checked his features through a magnifying lens. Grey-haired and sixtyish, there was a slight dip to the right side of his mouth, which could have indicated a recent stroke. I checked the left eye. By the way the lid drooped, the eye was obviously false. No doubt about it.

Shortly afterward, when I reentered Hawk's office, he leaned back in his creaky chair, a couple of inches of dead cigar screwed into a corner of his mouth.

"All right," he rasped. "What're your views on Salobin now?"

"Incredible," I replied. "Salobin's got to be our best pipeline inside Russia to date."

"Not anymore," Hawk shot back. "Whatever value Salobin's been to us is gone. Finished! At least that's where things stand at this moment. The man has vanished. Disappeared without a trace. Now listen carefully while I fill you in."

Briefly, Hawk ticked off the points.

Only two weeks before, according to Salobin's American controller, the aging missile expert had shown increasing signs of restlessness. Fed up with his country's stranglehold on the minds and lives of its citizens, Salobin told his U.S. controller that he had decided to make his defection complete and leave Russia for good and come over to the West. An important scientific conference was scheduled to be held in Tiflis, a southeastern Russian city not far from the Turkish border, and Salobin's plan was to attend the conference and, at an opportune moment, slip over into Turkey.

"And he actually pulled it off," Hawk concluded. "He used some kind of disguise, and he had a set of forged traveling papers on him when his train stopped at the border for the usual inspection. Once on the other side, Salobin boarded a Turkish train headed for Istanbul. But he never arrived."

"Maybe he never did get on the train."

Hawk shook his head. "He got on it all right, because the people handling things on our side, at least, had the good sense to put a spotter aboard the Turkish train. Salobin was seen getting on, and again when the train stopped at Ordu along the Turkish coast. But there were two other stops during the night, and this is where our spotter becomes vague. Although he's convinced that Salobin remained in his compartment, he wasn't in it when the train pulled into Istanbul the following morning."

"It could have been the Russians," I suggested. "Maybe they had caught on to Salobin's plan to defect and came after him. Since the train made two stops during the night, they could've managed to get him off and then beat it back to their own border."

"Exactly my own thoughts at first," Hawk said. "But I had to change my mind when I received this last night."

Sifting through some papers on his cluttered desk, he came up with a teletype transmitted in AXE's 4-x code. It bore a Lebanon dispatch point and it was rubber stamped CRITICALLY URGENT. Hawk had already run it through the decoder, and he filled me in.

The message had been dispatched by Salobin's former American controller and it was a blunt cry for help. Through a reliable underground informant, the American intelligence agent had received a tip that Salobin's whereabouts might be learned if a person in a position of authority would contact a man by the name of Rafai at the Club Salah in Beirut.

"It could be something, or maybe nothing," Hawk pointed out. "I've already checked the Interpol file and they list this Rafai as a lower level international hit man who deals in drugs, stolen goods, prostitution—anything that can be turned into a quick buck. But considering Salobin's importance, Rafai will have to be checked out."

Hawk paused to relight his cigar. After blowing out the match he shook his head wearily. "It may not be fair to criticize some of the other services who share our kind of work, but you know how it is, Nick. After they foul things up, they usually come knocking on AXE's door to bail them out. And when that happens I generally end up calling on you. Right?"

This was about as far as the old man had ever gone in paying me a compliment, and there was only one way to thank him.

"How soon do you want me to leave for Beirut?" I asked.

For a moment I thought he was going to smile, but

he made a point of clearing his throat suddenly and scowled at his watch. "You're booked to fly out of Dulles in about two hours. That'll give you just about enough time to pack a few things."

When I reached the door, he called out. His pale, blue eyes were deadly serious. "There are people high up in our government watching this one, Nick. They want Salobin. They place the highest value on his specialized knowledge. If Salobin's still among the living I want you to bring him in alive. I don't care how you do it, or how many you may have to kill to get the job done. But just do it. And the faster the better."

The first leg of my flight took me to Rome, and after an hour layover I continued directly to Lebanon aboard a Middle East Airline flight. After arriving at Beirut's International Airport, I had the baggage clerk send my luggage on to the Hotel Saint Georges and then I grabbed a cab for the ride into town.

Beirut is a cosmopolitan city, and though Arabic is the official language French and English are widely spoken. My cabbie spoke all three. Sometimes almost simultaneously. By the time he dropped me in front of the Club Salah I knew he was married, had four kids and that he moonlighted as a pastry chef when he wasn't pushing his cab.

And that's how I happened to find myself seated in the rear booth of a grimy Beirut bar, tired, and in no way knowing what to expect.

Frankly, I had no game plan in mind. Hawk had said it right. The Rafai lead could easily turn out to be nothing, a time-consuming false alarm. Meanwhile, as the minutes dragged by, the redhead at the bar kept swiveling around on her barstool to flash me one of her come-on smiles. I didn't encourage her but a bit later she got up, walked right past my booth and disappeared behind a beaded curtain at the far end of the room. I snuffed out my cigarette, lit up a fresh one, and then the beaded curtain parted and three musicians filed out, a drummer and two men carrying stringed instruments. They got a mild round of applause from the crowd as they took their places on the small bandstand.

They spent a few minutes tuning up, while the customers showed signs of growing impatience. The clapping grew louder and some foot stomping joined in. Moments later the hand drummer started the beat, and when the strings joined in, the beaded curtain parted a second time. The applause was deafening when the redhead glided into view.

Barefoot, she wore a pair of hip-hugging harem pants that revealed warm tints of pink flesh beneath the wispy fabric. A rainbow colored sash covered with flashing spangles draped her arching breasts, and as she picked up the throbbing rhythm her rotating stomach became the focal point for every male eye in the room. As the tempo quickened, so did the redhead's movements.

Over and over she kept circling the room, and the hand clapping, cheering customers roared approval. About the eighth or ninth time around she stopped before my booth, her hips flashing wildly as the music soared to crescendo level. Seconds later the music and the girl came to an explosive halt.

After acknowledging the cheers and applause, she turned to me and smiled. "You American," she said a bit breathlessly. "I know just by looking. When I smile, you do nothing. But when I dance," and her eyes sparkled wickedly, "you watch very careful. So now maybe you buy Hananna drink—yes?"

Flipping an arm around my neck she squirmed onto my lap, and that's when the big guy in the booth on the opposite side of the dance floor let out a howl.

This was one kind of trouble I didn't need. "Look," I told her. "You're getting your boyfriend nervous. You talk nice to him and I'll have the waiter bring both of you a drink. Anything you like."

Glaring at the big guy over her shoulder, she stuck her tongue out at him and then turned back to me. "He no boyfriend. He fat pig. But I like tall American like you. You be Hananna's boyfriend, yes?"

Giggling, she leaned closer, pressed her lips to mine and gave me a quick taste of her tongue.

That did it. Suddenly the big guy was on his feet, lunging our way. I pushed her off me and managed to get out of the booth as he closed in, his curved fingers going for my eyes. I caught his hand and pressed back on the thumb all the way. There was a dry, snapping sound and he let out a cry of pain. Tossing his hand aside, I backhanded him across the mouth and blood spurted from his torn lip. He let out another howl and charged. I side-stepped, hit him with the flat edge of my right hand alongside his neck. He grunted, his head flopping forward as his eyes glazed over. He hit the floor, knees first and slid forward on his face.

Some chairs scraped. For a while it looked like the beginning of a free-for-all, but the whole thing came to an abrupt halt as three men barged into the crowd, slapping at anyone who got in their way.

When the big guy on the floor struggled to a sitting position, one of the newcomers shouted at him in Arabic and then turned to me.

He was medium height, had a pockmarked complexion, and with his dark suit and lemon yellow tie he looked as if he had stepped straight out of a 1940 "Bogey" movie.

"My name Rafai," he snapped. He nodded toward the beaded doorway. "You come. We talk."

CHAPTER 2

"The eye is bigger than the belly," says an old Arab proverb, and Rafai's eyes had a very hungry look.

We sat facing each other across a small table in the rear room, with Rafai's two men posted at the doorway. There was a bottle of scotch and two glasses on the table, but when he offered to pour me a drink I shook my head. I wanted to keep it strictly business. The Lebanese are shrewd traders. They come by it through centuries of tradition, and I figured Rafai to be a first class pro.

By way of openers, I bluntly told him that I held a position of some authority in my government, and that word had come to us that he may be able to supply us with information about an individual my people were interested in locating.

"Am I correct so far?" I asked.

Rafai grinned, showing a lot of gold teeth. Reaching inside his jacket pocket he took out a small photograph and placed it in front of me. It looked as if it had been taken with a Poloroid camera, and the man in the picture certainly looked like Salobin. When I examined it close up I was even more positive. There was the same dip to the right side of the mouth, and there was no mistaking the false left eye.

I casually tossed the picture back and poker-faced it as best I could. "It could be the right man," I admitted, "but a picture is still a picture. It's the man I'm interested in."

Rafai's grin broadened. "But of course. And the man, he is close by."

"How close?"

Rafai shrugged. "Later, later. What matter now is if you have interest."

I was interested of course, but I was trying to pry loose whatever information I could. "You say he's close by," I repeated, "but we know for a fact that he disappeared in Turkey, and now you're saying he's here in Lebanon. How do you explain that?"

"I explain nothing," he shot back. "I not have to. So I repeat. Have you interest?"

It was back to me. "Interested. Now if you have any information, I'm prepared to—"

"What I have better than information," he interrupted. "I have man."

The surprise must have shown in my eyes. Grinning smugly, Rafai leaned forward, picked up the bottle of scotch and poured himself a drink. He took his time. After swishing it around, he tossed it down in a single gulp and then carefully put the empty glass down. The room had become very silent. I let it stay that way. I wanted him to come to me. The seconds slipped by. He wiped his mouth with the back of his hand and leaned back, the chair creaking under his weight.

"So now," he finally smirked. "Like I tell you, I have man. And you have interest. Good. So now we talk price, yes?"

"How much?"

He chuckled and held up one hand. "Five hundred thousand *American* dollars."

"You've got to be joking," I chuckled back.

"Rafai no joke," he snapped, and the smile vanished. "That is price. If too much, I find others. Maybe I speak to Russians. Maybe even Chinese."

He unbuttoned his jacket, hooked his thumbs in his belt and waited.

I knew that Rafai was speaking from a position of strength and I was rather certain that he knew that I knew it, too. It reasoned out that if he really did have Salobin—and I was beginning to think he did—then he'd have no trouble selling him to the Russians who would be only too glad to have Salobin back.

And he could be right about the Chinese, too. With Peking straining to develop a missile delivery system for their growing nuclear arsenal, Salobin's knowledge could readily provide the know-how they might still lack. The fact that Salobin might not volunteer the information wouldn't count for much once Mao's boys got to work on him. One way or another they'd manage to wring what they needed from the kidnapped Russian.

While I continued to mull these thoughts around, Rafai became impatient. "Well?" he demanded. "We talk price? Yes or no?"

I refused to be rushed. "Look," I said, "so far all I've seen is a picture. I'll need more than that to convince my people before they'd pay that kind of money."

For the first time Rafai's eyes showed some uncertainty. "Maybe I make mistake," he rasped. "Maybe we forget whole thing."

I was sure he was bluffing, so I decided to tough it through. "If you have the right man, and if he's alive, there's a good chance the money could be raised. But that means I'll have to see the man first. It's a condi-

tion I know my people will insist upon. Either we agree
on this, or we're wasting each other's time."

Indicision flickered in his eyes, and swinging to his
feet he went into a close huddle with his two men.
They spoke in low whispers, and it was impossible to
follow them. After a while they began to raise their
voices. Shouting back, Rafai bellowed them into
silence.

"Okay," he said, turning back to me. "We take you
to see man. But not now."

"How soon?"

"One day. Maybe two. We see."

I would have liked a definite time, but I didn't press.
Getting out my pocket pad I wrote down the name of
my hotel, and underneath it, Lee Perrin, the cover
name AXE had assigned me before leaving. Tearing
off the sheet, I gave it to Rafai.

When we left the room I spotted Hananna seated at
the end of the bar. She had changed back to her low-
necklined dress. She saw me, started forward, but
Rafai let out a growl and she hopped back on the barstool like a circus seal. Rafai offered me a ride, but I
refused.

Moments later I pushed my way through the crowd
and out into the humid, noisy street.

CHAPTER 3

I didn't sleep well that night. For one thing, I dreamed I was back in Hawk's Washington office and he was chewing me out for having fouled up the mission. While this was going on, Hananna suddenly materialized in her harem pants costume and when Hawk spluttered and came close to swallowing his cigar, the girl broke out in a wild, hip-flinging dance that drove the old man right up the wall. While he yelled and threatened to throw us both out, the phone started to ring. Only this wasn't in the dream.

Forcing myself awake, I slipped the phone off the cradle. It was the hotel desk clerk calling to tell me that my baggage had arrived from the airport. Did I want it sent up right away? I told him yes, and then had him switch me to room service.

A moment later the girl's husky, sensual voice hummed in my ear. *"Sahbah kheyr."*

I returned the greeting and plunged right on. *"Aseer bur tuam, beyd masslook."*

20

It was a simple request for orange juice and eggs, but she spotted my American accent instantly.

"Orange juice and eggs," she repeated in what sounded like British English. "Very good, sir. And how would you like your eggs?"

"Medium boiled." I felt vaguely disappointed. I would have liked continuing with Arabic, but decided to go with the tide. "And I'll want some toast and lots of coffee. And make sure the coffee's hot. *Very* hot."

"Of course, sir," she said in what sounded like a miffed tone, and clicked off.

The baggage came up while I was brushing my teeth. The bellhop was bilingual and all smiles. After he put the luggage on the rack at the foot of the bed, he immediately told me that he could provide me with any number of interesting female companions if I were in the mood. I declined, tipped him and sent him packing.

Ten minutes later breakfast arrived. The waiter, also bilingual, briskly transferred the food from his wheeled cart to the table in front of the large window that faced the sea. When he finished, he offered the same pitch the bellhop had given me. I refused, tipped him, but he hung in there, peddling his wares like a door-to-door salesman. Taking him firmly by the arm I led him out.

Grinning, I sat down to breakfast. I'm a reasonable man, but when it comes to clothes and women I do my own selecting. It's a rule. Another rule is that I don't pay hard cash for the intimate pleasures of female companionship. Handing over money would simply destroy it for me. Maybe that makes me old-fashioned, but I intend to stay this way until I'm ninety-five. After that, I'll play it strictly by ear.

The eggs were perfect, the coffee scalding hot. While I ate I went over my meeting with Rafai. For a while I thought I'd give Hawk a call and fill him in. He had given me two "clean" phones I could use in Beirut, including the one in the U.S. Consulate, but while I lingered over my second cup of coffee and a cigarette I decided to hold off.

At the moment I still had nothing definite to report. So far I had seen a picture of someone who may have been Salobin, but was that enough? And there was Rafai to consider. The man was a known crook, which made his credibility more than suspect. It was also possible that Rafai may have simply gotten his hands on a picture of Salobin and was pushing for all he could get. Whether he'd still contact me was something I couldn't be sure of. Accordingly, I decided to play it like it was, keep my own counsel for the time being and hopefully wait for Rafai to get in touch as he had promised.

For the rest of the morning, and right through late afternoon, I remained in my room. If Rafai wanted to reach me, I didn't want to miss him. To break the monotony I watched TV and had the unsettling experience of seeing a Bonanza re-run with an Arabic soundtrack dubbed in. Before dinner, I ducked out for a newspaper at one of the foreign newstands on *Rue Hamra,* the Beirut equivalent of 42nd Street. The sidewalk was jammed with people, the street snarled with bumper-to-bumper traffic.

A lot of Arab oil money flows into Beirut, and I guess it's one of the few cities in the world where a Silver Cloud Rolls and a donkey-drawn cart will stop side-by-side while waiting for the light to turn green. In the few minutes it took me to walk to and from my hotel, I saw this happen no less than four times.

When I returned to the hotel I went directly to the desk, but no one had tried to reach me. I spent the next ten minutes in the lobby cocktail lounge nursing an oversized Tom Collins. The waitress, a tall, attractive girl with sad, thoughtful eyes and a warm smile came by twice to check my drink. Her smile was open to any number of interpretations, but that's as far as I let it go.

That evening I had dinner in my room, watched some more TV, and finished things off by browsing through the Paris edition of the *Tribune* I had picked up at the stand. At a little past eleven, with still no word from Rafai, I set the air conditioner on low, slipped into a pair of pajama bottoms and got into bed. I had no trouble falling asleep. I must have dropped off within seconds after my head hit the feathers.

The following morning was a repeat of the day before. After some breakfast, I spent a leisurely hour with Wilhelmina, my 9mm Luger. I took it apart slowly and methodically, lubricated the various parts and then carefully wiped off the excess oil before reassembling it. I was simply killing time. When I finally replaced Wilhelmina in my shoulder holster it was getting on to eleven.

There's a lot of waiting in my kind of work, and though you get used to it, you never get *that* used to it, either. What I didn't like, and it was something I had to consider, was that Rafai could have decided to talk with either the Russians or the Chinese after all. And if he had, and if a bargain had been struck with one or the other, it could mean that I had already been dealt out.

The thought of being left swinging in the breeze depressed me. For a while I was again tempted to get in touch with Hawk, but I again ruled it out. He was 5,000 miles away, and the moves had to be all mine.

Something's bound to pop, I kept telling myself, and oddly enough it was just around here when the phone rang. It was the desk clerk telling me that I had a caller waiting in the lobby.

"Shall I tell him you will be down, sir?"

"Right away," I replied, and hung up fast.

After slinging the shoulder holster in place, I slipped into my jacket. When I checked myself in the dresser mirror, the Luger's slight bulge scarcely showed. Satisfied, I left the room, locked up, and instead of taking the elevator I walked down the four flights. When I entered the lobby I spotted Rafai right off. He stood at the far end of the desk, and when our eyes met he nodded briefly, turned, and made straight for the revolving doors. I followed right behind him.

A black Mercedes was parked at the curb, and as Rafai approached it the rear door swung open. He held it open and stepped aside when I came up. One of the men who had been with Rafai at the Club Salah was seated in the rear, and the second man was behind the wheel. After I climbed in, Rafai slid in beside me. I didn't like being sandwiched between Rafai and his goon, but it wasn't a matter of choice. Moments after Rafai pulled the door shut behind him, the driver shifted into gear and the Mercedes eased its way into the stream of traffic.

"You took your time getting back to me," I said matter-of-factly. "Everything all right?"

Rafai shrugged and remained silent.

I took the cue and buttoned up.

At the corner the driver took a right turn, drove another block and made a left. Two blocks further on he made another right. After a few more turns I was no longer sure where we were. At intervals, Rafai twisted around in his seat and looked out the rear window, obviously checking if I'd put a tail on him. I hadn't, of course, but there was no point telling him since he wouldn't believe me anyway. So I sat there silently as the driver turned and zigzagged through a maze of twisting, narrow streets.

Finally we were out in the open, moving along a broad boulevard lined with luxury high-rise apartment buildings that faced the sparkling blue sea. Suddenly, we were out of the city, and I figured the heading to be east since the sea was no longer visible through Rafai's side window. A few minutes later Rafai muttered something to the driver and he eased down on the brakes, coming to a smooth park alongside the shoulder.

Twisting around in his seat, Rafai took another long look through the rear window. Traffic was light, and after a few cars swished by he turned back and held out his hand, palm up. His voice was calm and businesslike.

"Your gun. I give back later. After we see man."

With Rafai's goon pressing something small, hard and round against my ribs, there wasn't much point in arguing. Reaching inside my jacket, I removed Wilhelmina and placed the luger in Rafai's open palm. After he slipped the gun into his jacket pocket, Rafai gave me a quick frisk, running his hands along my sides and then down my legs, but he failed to discover Hugo, the thin stiletto I kept in a special chamois sheath strapped to my arm. Satisfied, he leaned back and told the driver to get going.

Pulling out, the driver turned left at the next corner, then straight on. It was obvious we were heading back toward the city. Ten minutes later we were back in Beirut's native quarter, moving at a snail's pace in the bumper-to-bumper traffic. We kept going down one street after another, and at one point, after making endless turns, I couldn't be sure if we had gone around the same block a half-dozen times. Finally, with unexpected suddenness, Rafai ordered the driver to stop in front of a dirty, narrow alley. Unlocking the Mercedes door, Rafai got out and motioned me to follow.

When I stepped out, the smell of raw sewage, cooking odors and rotting garbage hit me like a punch in the gut. Rafai moved ahead of me, slapping away at the outstretched arms of jabbering peddlers and beggars who suddenly clustered around us. I stayed close, with Rafai's two goons bringing up the rear.

Pushing and shoving, Rafai finally scattered the crowd and led the way to a four-story tenement at the far end of the alley. The building's windows that faced the street were boarded up, and it looked as if it had been abandoned a long time.

Rafai pointed to a short flight of stone steps that led to the basement. "We go here," he said impatiently.

I followed him down, his two goons close behind. Just beyond the steps we halted before the basement door. Rafai pounded on it, waited a few seconds and pounded again.

Footsteps approached. A muffled voice called out from inside, and Rafai barked back. There was a pause, followed by the click of a lock being turned. When the door opened a crack, Rafai pushed against it and we all followed him into a narrow, long hallway illuminated by a single, naked overhead bulb. The man who had opened the door relocked it, and he whispered something to Rafai. Rafai nodded, and again led the way.

It was a hideous scene. Paint and plaster flaked from the walls and ceiling and a constant scratching sound came from inside the walls. The rat population had to be enormous. Rooms lined each side of the hallway, and we passed a sagging staircase that vanished into the darkness above. At the end of the hall Rafai stopped before a closed door. Turning the knob, he swung it open. Stepping aside, he waved me in.

The only piece of furniture in the room was a large brass bed. On it lay a slightly built, elderly man, his face turned to the wall. When I stood beside the bed, stared down, he stirred and turned his head in my direction. The small, overhead bulb threw more shadows than light, and when I bent over for a better look his eyelids fluttered open. He mumbled something, but the incoherent, vowel sounds didn't form words.

Getting out my pencil flashlight, I thumbed the switch and aimed the narrow beam at his right eye. Despite the concentrated light, the pupil remained fully dilated and didn't contract in the least. I switched to the left eye. There was no response either, but for a good reason. The eye was false.

"Well," Rafai grunted when I straightened up. "This is right man—yes?"

It was Salobin all right. The plastic left eye had convinced me completely, but his disoriented state had me worried.

"What the hell have you been pumping into him?" I demanded.

Rafai shrugged. "Something to help old man sleep. It go away."

His beady eyes searched mine. "Now that you see man, we talk business."

He was eager to wrap it up, and the only move I could make at the moment was to stall for time.

"Of course I'll have to get in touch with my people first. I'll tell them what you want, and then it's up to them."

He scowled. It was obvious he didn't like it one damn bit. "How long this take?"

"Three, maybe four days. But remember, we're talking about a lot of money."

Still scowling, he walked over to where his two men stood with their backs against the closed door. After a brief, whispered huddle, he came back to me.

"We give three days to finish business, make deal. No more. You agree?"

I had to nod, and the meeting was over.

Turning, Rafai ordered one of his men at the door to open up. He grabbed the knob and pulled, but it seemed to be stuck. He gave another pull, a really hard one, and the door swung open. A split second later he let out a startled cry. The burst of gunfire followed instantly. The guy who had opened the door caught it head on. Slammed off his heels, he rocketed back into the room, bowling over the man who stood behind him.

I dove for Salobin and managed to yank him off the bed. There was a door in the corner, either a closet or leading into another room. Bullets thudded into the

wall and pinged off the brass bedstead as I dragged
Salobin across the floor. I just about made it, reached
for the knob, but that's as far as I got. Suddenly, something hard slapped me heavily behind my left ear. I
struggled to stay up, but my legs weren't getting the
message.

I went down slowly while the shooting went on and
on. Finally, gratefully, the darkness closed in and
blotted out the pain.

CHAPTER 4

I came to hearing the girl's voice. Gradually, I focused on the blurred but somewhat familiar features. It took a few more seconds to match the voice with the face.

"Hananna . . .?"

"Yes, Hananna," she whispered.

She knelt beside me, tugging at my arm and trying to get me to my feet. There was still a lot of pain in my head.

"Please," she insisted. "Get up. I help. But hurry . . ."

I managed to hook an arm around her shoulder and wobbled to my feet. I was wondering how the hell she had happened to turn up, and then my thoughts leaped to Salobin. The room was littered with corpses, but Salobin wasn't one of them.

"The old man," I muttered. "Where is he?"

"Some men take him away," she replied. "But we not talk now. We hurry. Come with Hananna, please . . ."

She pulled at my arm, but I still hung back. Gradually, I took in the scene. It was a blood bath. The guy who had caught the first burst lay on his back, his features smashed beyond recognition. Alongside him was his buddy, lying face down, the back of his head soaked with blood. The man who let us in had taken numerous bullets in the chest, and Rafai lay at the foot of the bed, his face obliterated beneath a veil of clotted blood.

It had to be the work of pros. It figured that their orders not only included the snatching of Salobin, but the liquidation of Rafai and his men, as well. While I stared, fighting back the pain inside my head, the inevitable question hit me.

Why not me . . .? Four men dead, but one is left alive. There had to be a reason. A good one.

Meanwhile, Hananna kept tugging at my arm. I was about ready to go, but stopped at the door. I had almost forgotten.

"Wait," I told her.

I crossed the room, knelt beside Rafai. Reaching inside his jacket pocket, I removed Wilhelmina and replaced the luger inside my shoulder holster. Moments later I rejoined the girl at the door. When we stepped into the hallway I noticed that the bulb had been turned off, but the front door was open a bit and a shaft of pale, yellow light illuminated the gloomy interior. I was still feeling groggy, but Hananna slipped her arm around my waist and we started forward. When we reached the door Hananna peeked out.

"It all right," she whispered. "Come."

After we stepped out into the noisy, sunlit street, Hananna pulled the heavy basement door shut. Her face was close to mine and her dark eyes, serious with concern, searched mine.

"You feel all right? Not hurt too much?"

"All right," I echoed.

"You sure?"

I nodded.

She grinned and kissed me lightly on the cheek.

"Good. I go get cab. We go to my place. But you wait here. You promise?"

I nodded again and leaned back against the door for support. She ran up the short flight of stone steps. At the top she turned. "You wait," she called back. "You promise."

Seconds later she was lost in the passing crowd.

For a while I didn't know which way to play it. My legs still felt rubbery, but the pain in my head had started to ease off. I carefully touched the spot behind my ear with the tips of my fingers and they came away with a few flakes of dried blood. Whoever had sapped me knew how to use a blackjack, and I was grateful. If he had swung a bit harder, or at a slightly different angle, I could have become a permanent resident of the basement, along with the rats and the four corpses.

So far I had been lucky. And that brought me back to Hananna and the fact that she had found me the way she did. But it was also disturbing. It meant she had to be involved in some way with what had happened. But how involved? Was it possible that she knew who the killers were? Was she a member of their team? In fact, getting me back to her place might have been some kind of plot. When I asked her how she came to be in the building she had put me off. Why?

The nagging questions kept coming, but there was something else to consider that outweighed everything else. Salobin had been kidnapped for a second time and Rafai was dead. With both of them gone, only the girl remained a possible, connecting link. I knew I would have to go with her. She was all I had left to work with.

Less than ten minutes later Hananna suddenly reappeared from out of the crowd. I managed my way up the steps and she quickly slipped her arm around my waist.

"Aha, you no go away," she smiled. "You keep promise. You make Hananna very happy."

The cab was waiting at the end of the alley, and after we got in she gave the driver an address. As we moved into the flow of traffic, she patted my hand.

"It not far," she smiled. "We be there soon."

Hananna's small, top-floor apartment was on the *Rue Ghalgoul,* a narrow street along the fringe of the native quarter. The first thing she did after settling me in a comfortable chair was clean the gash in my scalp. She did a good job, using a cloth soaked in alcohol, and continually stopping to ask if she were hurting me. When she finished, she brought me a small glass of *arrack,* a kind of brandy, and then propped a big satin pillow behind my head and insisted that I relax. She left me and disappeared into the small bedroom.. When she came out a few minutes later she was wearing a clinging blue robe and matching mules. There was no bra under the robe. I could tell that by the way the cloth outlined the nipples underneath. With her thick, red hair spilling across her shoulders she looked absolutely smashing.

She refilled my glass and vanished again, this time to the kitchen. Pots and pans rattled noisily and eventually she returned with a steaming bowl of *kibbeh,* a dish of lamb mixed with rice and wheat kernals. She apologized for the fact that it was made from leftovers, but it was absolutely delicious.

Up until now I had held back from questioning her, but with the meal finished, and facing her across the small table, I figured the moment of truth had arrived. Lighting up a cigarette, I leaned back in my chair.

"Hananna," I began, "there are certain things I must know—questions that need answering. And I think you can help me."

She squirmed uncomfortably in her chair and avoided looking at me. "You want to know how

Hananna come to that house. How she find you on floor. Is this not so?"

"Is so," I mimicked her.

She hesitated for a moment and her eyes met mine again. "I come to house because Rafai ask me. He ask me to do what you call, how you say, favor."

"What kind of favor?"

"To help old man. He sick, and Rafai ask me to bring food—to care for him. I feel sorry for this old man. This is truth. You believe Hananna. Yes?"

Her eyes had suddenly become moist and her voice trembled to the breaking point.

"I want to believe you," I said, "but four men were killed in that house, and the old man Rafai had asked you to look after is missing." I snuffed out the cigarette and put my hand over hers. "Something is frightening you," I continued, "and I want to help. But I can't unless you tell me everything and from the very beginning."

For a moment she hesitated, but when I gave her hand a gentle squeeze she began to talk, slowly at first, then more rapidly, as if she were eager to unburden herself of some feeling of guilt.

She explained how Rafai had gotten her the job at the Club Salah six months before. Things hadn't been going well for her at the time and Rafai had been kind. He had bought her clothes and some small gifts. She didn't go into their relationship beyond that, and I didn't ask. Then, about a week earlier, Rafai had come to her and asked her to look in on the old man.

"When Rafai bring me to house for first time," she continued, "I can tell old man is sick. He has fever, and he no eat. But I wash him, and when I feed him he eat a little. Sometimes he say something, a few words in English, sometimes in language I do not understand. But most time he just sleep."

"What about Rafai?" I asked. Didn't he tell you

something about the old man? Who he was? Why he was in this empty house?"

Hananna's eyes brightened momentarily. "But sure he tell me. Rafai say old man is friend, but that he hide from police. When I ask why he hide, he say it big secret. He tell me not to talk of old man to anybody. He also promise me money, many more pounds than I make dancing. So I come each day to house. I feed old man, wash him. Do little things, and not just for money but because I am sorry for him."

"And how long did you do this?"

"Three, four days. Maybe five. Rafai tell me brother of old man come soon, take him someplace else." She shrugged, and the fear was back in her eyes. "I am scared that old man hide from police. Maybe, I think, this make big trouble for Hananna. But Rafai say I must do this favor, so I do." She stopped speaking and looked at me directly. "You know old man?" she asked. "Is what Rafai say about old man so?"

I let her questions slide by. "What about today?" I pressed. "Tell me everything that happened once you got to the house."

She hesitated and licked her lips. "All right, I tell. When I come to house today, Hamid—he is one who stay with old man all time—let me in. Hamid surprised because I come always with Rafai. But now I alone."

"Why?"

"I worry, that why. Day before, old man not good. I feel sorry. So I come early. Not wait for Rafai. I bring dish of *kibbeh* and some wine. Same like you just eat. The old man very tired. He hardly talk. But I give him some *kibbeh*, a little wine. I think he feel little better. But, before I go, this knock on front door. It is Rafai. I afraid Rafai be angry that I come to house alone. So I ask Hamid he please not tell Rafai. So I go quick into empty room in hall, close door . . ."

She paused. It was obviously getting tougher for her as she came closer to the end.

"What happened next?" I asked gently.

She took a deep breath, exhaled. "When Hamid let Rafai in, I look through small hole in old door. Then I see you, too. I much surprised. I do not know why you there. You cannot be brother of old man. You *Amricanee!* I all mixed up in head. I am also—how you say—scared. So when you, Rafai and others go into room of old man and close door, I wait very still. I like very much to go away, but am not able. If I go, I must open front door, open lock. If I open lock, Rafai find out and Hananna in big trouble. So I no go. I have need to wait. I cannot go before Rafai go away first. That is so, yes?"

I nodded. So far her story hung together. "So you waited," I said. "And then . . .?"

"I hear sound. First I think maybe it be rats. But I look through hole in door and it not rats. It men. Three. They come down stairs. Very slow, careful."

"They were coming down," I interrupted. A sudden thought hit me. "Do the stairs go to the roof? Is there a door to the roof?"

"Sure there door," she replied quickly. "That is way they come. They do not come front door. That is truth."

It was perfectly plausible. Since the house was attached to the other buildings on the block it would have been a simple matter for the killers to have entered an adjoining building, and then come down by way of the roof door.

"What about the hall light?" I asked. "One of them must have turned it off."

"Is so," she replied quickly. "I see one man reach up, turn light off. It dark now and I very scared. I also very still. I wait. Not know what to do. Then . . ."

Her hands flew to her ears.

"The shooting began?"

She nodded quickly. "Much shooting. Much, much noise. Then it stop. All very quiet now. I wait. Not move. Not even breathe. Soon I hear sound. Men speaking. Again I look through hole in door. Only now I no see. It very dark. But soon I hear old man voice. He holler something. They have old man. I am sure. I hear front door open. I wait. When no more sound come, I leave room . . ."

She stood up and went to the window. I waited. When she began speaking again her back was to me, her voice scarcely above a whisper.

"When I go to room where old man was, I see Rafai . . . dead. I see others dead, too. I see you. I think you dead. But you move . . . make sound. So I come by you. Help best I can . . ."

I went over to where she stood and put my hands gently on her shoulders. She turned slowly. The tears in her eyes gave her a childlike, innocent look.

"I believe you, Hananna," I said. "And I owe you so much. For your honesty. For your help."

I kissed her on the forehead, a purely reassuring gesture. She smiled, touched her lips lightly to mine. She did it a second time, only now her soft, moist lips parted and her tongue glided into my mouth. A spark was suddenly kindled, and became a flame.

When we broke for air her deep brown eyes searched mine. The look of the child was gone, replaced by the sensual eloquence of a passionate, mature woman.

Cupping my face in her slender hands, she began moving her lips back and forth across my mouth, light brushing strokes that set every nerve in my body tingling. The flame quickly became a roaring blaze. I found the bowed sash of her robe and gave one of the ends a gentle tug. It untied instantly and the filmy garment drifted open. Her pear-shaped breasts sprang into view, the erect nipples a shade darker than the surrounding flesh.

I swept the robe aside, and when my hands moved down over her smooth, rounded buttocks, she gave a cry of joy and pressed her hot, moist mouth against my neck. I scooped her up in my arms and carried her into the bedroom. Gently, I eased her onto the large bed.

The pleasurable things in life pass much too quickly, and making love is one of them. But I was determined to play it slowly, to prolong these precious moments both for myself and her. I kissed her throat, lingered over her shoulders. As I moved lower, she cupped her breasts in her hands and gave another little cry of pleasure when I flicked my tongue across one nipple. Gently, I encircled it with my mouth, drew upon it. Her body trembled, arched.

"*Maluh, maluh,*" she moaned in Arabic. Beautiful, beautiful.

I continued to kiss, caress, to probe and explore. Her passion took wings. I touched her thighs with my fingertips. It was only a touch, but they parted instantly, making room for my searching hand. I plunged deeply within her thighs, moving upward along the satin smooth flesh until her soft mound nestled snug and moist beneath my palm. She groaned, strained and cried out as I manipulated the quivering flesh with every bit of skill I possessed. Suddenly, a powerful ecstatic ripple raced through her body.

"Now," she pleaded. "*Now . . .*"

I unzipped, getting out of my pants and shorts in nothing flat. I had been long ready, but when she slid under me and grasped my manhood, positioning it to her liking, it took every bit of restraint I had to keep from bursting.

"Soon," she whispered close to my ear. "Soon."

Her rhythm began—slow enticing rotations that sent shock wave after shock wave pounding through me. It's impossible to know when a sensation ends and another begins, but suddenly she was opening to me. Flesh yielded to flesh. Gradually, her dancer's legs moved upward, her heels brushing my calves. Her pelvis arched as she drew me in fully and completely. Her legs locked and our thrusting began—savage, lightning strokes that matched the wild beating of our hearts. We rode the long, sweeping wave in. Sounds filled the room. Strange sounds. Our sounds. It went on for a long time, the sounds and the movements conjoining, becoming one until the wave finally broke, swept over us and moved on.

For a few moments we lay there, breathing heavily, stunned by the incredible intensity of the experience. Slowly, her legs untwined, released me. Easing up, I rolled off, drew her close.

She didn't speak.

Dusk showed beyond the window. A single star, like a chip of polished diamond, glittered in the darkening sky.

"Do not go," she finally whispered. "Stay with Hananna."

Her hand guided mine beneath the sheet.

"I stay," I whispered back.

CHAPTER 5

Sunlight flooding the room awakened me. I blinked and reached out. Hananna was no longer beside me, but I heard her a moment later, humming in the kitchen. As I swung my feet over the side of the bed, she entered the room smiling radiantly and wearing the same robe she had worn the night before. I vividly recalled the treasures it hid and felt familiar stirrings when she brushed her lips lightly across mine.

"I make eggs," she smiled. "Big pan full. And coffee. Like you like, I hope."

She patted my cheek briefly and hurried back to the kitchen.

I dressed quickly, checked my face in the oval mirror above the small vanity. I needed a shave, but it would have to wait. I joined Hananna in the kitchen and found the coffee and scrambled eggs waiting. We ate facing each other, experiencing the magical afterglow that comes to a man and woman who have shared each other for the first time.

Suddenly she gave a little giggle. "It is funny thing. Last night we make beautiful love. We are together like one. But many things I do not know. Like who you are? Why you come to house with Rafai? Or why you have gun?" Her brow puckered. "Is it you hide from police, too? Like old man?"

I knew she'd be asking me questions like these sooner or later, and though I felt she could be trusted, I was careful not to tell her more than was absolutely necessary. So far, all she knew about me was my cover name, and I knew I had to keep it that way. I did tell her, however, that I was not hiding from the police, and that neither was Salobin.

She seemed to be thinking this over as she refilled my emptied cup. "But now what happen? What happen if police find Rafai and others dead? They ask questions, yes? Maybe they come looking to Hananna for answer?"

Her hand trembled when she put the coffee pot down.

Actually, I didn't think this too likely. For one thing, the building was uninhabited, so it could be weeks before the bodies would be found. And by that time, considering the basement's rat population, the chances were there wouldn't be much to identify.

I put my hand over hers. "Don't worry," I said. "It will be all right. And please, trust me a little longer."

I got up and slipped my jacket from the back of the chair. In a moment she stood before me, her eyes searching mine.

"You go now?"

"I must."

"But you come back?"

I grinned. "Later this afternoon. Sooner if I can."

Beaming, she slipped her arms around me, pressing her face close to my chest. "I fix good dinner, and I no go to Club Salah tonight. Instead we make beautiful love again. Many times. Many different way. Yes?"

"Yes."

I kissed her at the door and stepped into the hall. When the door clicked shut behind me I hurried down the three flights of wooden stairs.

The first thing I did was to take a cab back to my hotel. I checked with the desk but there had been no messages. On the way up to my room in the elevator some of the perplexing questions of the day before returned. Uppermost was the fact that I hadn't been killed along with Rafai and his crew. It still troubled me while I showered and shaved. No matter how I turned it around it kept coming back to one thing. Professional killers wouldn't have spared me without a reason. This meant they would've been working under express orders. If so, from whom?

I wiped a dollop of shaving cream from my chin and left the bathroom. There was always the possibility that the killers could have been Russian agents. Perhaps members of the KGB. After all, it made sense that the Russians would have been hunting around by this time for Salobin, and if they had somehow tracked him to Rafai I could understand the basement slaughter in those terms. But knowing the way the Russians operate, my being left alive didn't add up. For one thing, Russian agents aren't in the habit of leaving loose ends lying around, especially when it might be a witness who could blow their cover. Accordingly, if the killers were Russians, they would've had to have an excellent reason for bypassing me and I couldn't even come up with a lousy one.

In fact, considering my on-going war with the Russians over the years, the liquidation of Nick Carter would have served their purposes beautifully. By getting rid of me they would be way ahead in the game.

After toweling myself dry, I dressed and took the elevator down. Minutes later I was in a cab, heading for the U.S. Consulate and a telephone call I didn't exactly look forward to making. Meanwhile, having temporarily shunted the Russians to one side, I faced a whole new line of inquiry. With the Russians ruled out, others had to be ruled in. Who? I was still chasing this one around, trying to find a likely angle that would throw some light on what might have been an answer, when the cab pulled up before the Consulate's driveway.

Minutes after I entered the building I was eyeball to eyeball with an attractive but persistant American receptionist.

"It just isn't done," she repeated. "You simply can't barge in and insist on seeing the attaché without an appointment."

I decided I'd do it the polite way first, figuring that honey would get me more. "But I'm *not* insisting. I'm merely requesting." I got out my wallet and removed one of AXE's cards with the cover name, "Amalgamated Press and Wire Service." "If you'll take this in to your First Attaché, I'm sure it will solve everything."

She took the card by one corner as though she were afraid of catching some disease. She gave it a quick glance and frowned. "Amalgamated Press and Wire Service? Are you a journalist?"

I shook my head.

"A reporter then?"

The sugar-coated treatment wasn't working, so I switched from Jekyll to Hyde. "Just bring it in now," I snapped. My smile was pure ice.

It worked. Her stylish glasses slid half-way down her pretty nose and her mouth popped open with surprise. For a second or two she seemed on the point of saying something, but she apparently changed her mind. She stood up, sniffed indignantly, and trotted off down a long carpeted hallway.

In a few minutes she was back, but accompanied by a middle-aged man who, all cordiality and smiles, introduced himself as Anthony J. Baylor, the Consulate's

First Attaché. The effect of this greeting on his receptionist was mildly amusing. Her glasses slipped again and her large brown eyes were a mix of bewilderment and awe as Baylor, grinning and nodding, led the way to his office.

Once in Baylor's office, I produced further indentification and requested use of the Consulate's scrambler phone. Taking me into a smaller, adjoining room, he pointed to the red instrument on a corner desk and discreetly left. Minutes later, the overseas operator was routing my call through. Seconds later, I heard the buzz of the phone on the other end. At the fourth ring there was a slight click as the phone was lifted from its cradle. Hawk's "Hello," grumpier and raspier than usual, followed.

I suddenly realized the time difference. It must have been three in the morning in D.C. and I cursed under my breath. Obviously the call had been transferred to his apartment and had gotten him up.

"N3 here," I said as cheerfully as I could.

There were some spluttering sounds, followed by some disgruntled throat clearing. Control finally returned. "All right, Nick. What's gone wrong?"

In deference to the old man I must say that he's a good listener. Patiently, I filled him in on the basement killings, plus everything else that had happened—except the intimate details involving Hananna and myself. I also aired my theory on possible Russian involvement and Hawk agreed that if the Russians had been involved I would never have been given the chance of leaving the basement.

"But expect them to move into the act at any time," he added quickly. "Meanwhile, you're sure about the old man you saw in the basement. It was Salobin?"

"Absolutely. His Russian was authentic and his plastic left eye clinched it."

"Then there's only the girl left to work with. Right? This dancer?"

"Right."

"And you believe she's telling you the truth?"

"Absolutely."

"Then you're going to have to go to work on her, Nick. I'm not suggesting she's holding out or anything, but she says she was at the house several times and she may have overheard bits of conversation between Rafai and his men—things she may have forgotten. Maybe some names were mentioned. An address. You'll have to get her to scratch her memory and get her to recall anything she may have noticed or heard during those visits. It could be nothing, but it could turn up something damned important, too. You agree?"

I grunted.

"And there's something else," he went on. "The people who snatched Salobin won't be sitting still. They'll be making other moves. So you'll have to be ready for anything."

I agreed again, and Hawk was wrapping things up.

"Then I guess that says about everything for the moment. Except that I'm sorry."

"About what?"

"About your getting that close to Salobin and having things misfire. By the way, how's your head feeling?"

"Better." I paused. "But I feel terrible about Salobin. I mean if—"

"Forget it, N3," he interrupted. "There's always another bus."

A second later he mumbled goodbye and clicked off.

When I hung up the flasher light winked off, signaling the end of the call and Baylor reentered the room almost immediately. I thanked him again, and he assured me that State was always happy to help out when they could. He let me out through a side door, and when I cut across the driveway and turned the corner onto the street it was a bit after twelve. I was anxious now to get back to Hananna's place, but there was something I wanted to do.

After flagging a cab, I had the driver take me back to *Rue Hamra,* Beirut's main shopping street. I got out on a corner opposite a huge neon sign and casually strolled along the crowded shop-lined street. The place is loaded with stalls packed with every kind of merchandise imaginable, but I finally saw what I wanted hanging in a jeweler's window—a string of handcrafted *misbaha* beads. The beads had a copperish tint and I figured they'd go beautifully with Hananna's red hair. I paid the shopkeeper exactly what he asked, even though I knew that he expected me to haggle. In a way, I didn't want to cheapen the gift.

By the time I left the shop and waved down another cab it was past one. I gave the cabbie Hananna's address, and as he eased into the heavy traffic my thoughts went back to the night before. Admittedly, my interest began to build. Some women merely give. Others give generously. Hananna definitely belonged to the second group.

About three blocks from Hananna's place, the traffic turned bumper-to-bumper and I refused to sweat it. I had the driver stop, pushed a pound note into his hand and hopped out.

I covered the remaining distance quickly. I remembered the small instrument shop at the corner of the *Rue Ghalgoul* and turned right into the alley-sized street. Hananna's apartment building was in the middle of the block and I couldn't help noticing the crowd clustered around the front steps. A moment later I spotted the ambulance parked at the curb, its siren wailing thinly.

I ran forward. Two old women at the edge of the crowd dabbed at their eyes. I asked in Arabic what was wrong, and they cried louder. A man alongside began to explain. He spoke quickly and I caught the words "knife" and "killers." All at once a collective groan went up from the crowd. Two ambulance attendants were bringing a litter out, and that's when my heart really began to pound. The body was completely covered by a sheet, but there was no mistaking the long red hair that spilled out from underneath. The crowd fell back, making room for the litter.

"Ilham'dilla," one of the old women sobbed. *God be praised.*

When the attendants raised the litter and began rolling it through the open doors of the ambulance, one of Hananna's lifeless arms slipped out from under the bloodstained sheet, swinging grotesquely back and forth.

Vaguely, I heard the doors thud shut. The siren's cry mounted and became a piercing scream.

CHAPTER 6

Death always takes us by surprise, and Hananna's had the impact of a bomb. Stunned, I watched the ambulance drive off. I was racked by rage, and felt an explosive urge to hit out and smash everything in sight. But gradually, as I walked the dirty, crooked streets, the rage subsided and gave way to mixed feelings of regret and remorse.

Hananna was the victim of her own innocence. Childlike, she had been drawn into a pattern of events beyond her depth. Like a fragile moth, she had been sucked into the flickering flame.

I also blamed myself. If I had stayed with her at the apartment, things might have gone differently. Her killer or killers would have had to deal with me. There could have been a different ending. She may have not had to die.

My mission still remained. It was my job, my work. Admittedly, as I reviewed the events, they were far from encouraging. Rafai was dead. Three of his men

were dead. Hananna was dead, and Salobin had disappeared for a second time. It was one hell of a box
score and though I felt committed to let Hawk know
about Hananna, I decided to hold off for the time
being. I had not only missed the bus once, but *twice*.
How many chances would the old man give me?

But through it all, the same nagging question kept
coming back. If all the others had been killed—why
not me?

There had to be an explanation, and I knew luck
had nothing to do with it. Of this I was convinced.

I must have done a lot of walking, because it was almost dusk when I found myself standing in front of my
hotel. When I checked with the desk clerk he had a
message. Someone had been trying to reach me. In
fact, the clerk said, the man had called four times.

"Did he leave his name? A number where he could
be reached?"

The clerk shook his head.

Obviously the pot was bubbling again, coming to a
fast boil.

I thanked the clerk, took my key, and headed for
the bank of elevators. I was about half-way there,
when the clerk called out. I turned. He held up the
phone, his palm covering the mouthpiece.

"The same man, sir."

"Give me a minute," I called back. "I'll take it in
my room."

I made it upstairs quickly and heard the phone ring
as I turned the key in the lock. Moments later I
snatched it off the cradle.

"Mr. Carter?"

The deep English-speaking voice had a distinct accent, but I couldn't place it. But the real surprise was
that he knew my name. Once your cover is blown
there's no point hedging and I didn't even try.

"You obviously know me," I replied. "Have we
met?"

He chuckled softly. "Not really, Mr. Carter, but I think it time we did. Perhaps I'd best introduce myself. My name is Janos Korla, and I must say straight off that I've heard a great deal about your skills and accomplishments. I think them very impressive."

Cheap flattery rubs my fur the wrong way. "Look, Korla," I said bluntly. "You haven't been trying to reach me all afternoon just to tell me you're a fan of mine. And the fact that you know who I am raises a hell of a lot of questions. So why not put it on the line. If you've got something to say to me, let's hear it."

There was a measured pause. "All right," he said evenly, but the smile was out of his voice. "Are you still interested in the Salobin matter?"

I felt my nerves starting to tingle. "Interested," I replied flatly.

"Then be at the Casino du Faune tomorrow evening at nine. A table will be waiting for you, reserved in my name."

Before I could reply, Janos Korla, whoever he was, clicked off.

CHAPTER 7

The Casino du Faune is about twenty miles north of Beirut, and it was a little past eight the following evening when I drove out of the city in my rented Mustang. I still hadn't called Hawk to give him the latest, but that afternoon I had put through a call to an old friend, Inspector Maurice Duval, an Interpol section chief who works out of Marseilles. I was interested in getting all the information I could on Janos Korla, and Duval promised to get back to me in an hour. It was somewhat less than that when he returned my call. The information he had was illuminating.

Duval described Korla as a *"grand poisson"*—a big fish. A Croat by birth, Korla had left his native Yugoslavia at the outbreak of World War II for London, but by the end of the war, and only thirty at the time, Korla had already amassed a sizable fortune as a wheeler-dealer in the flourishing penicillin black market. From here, Korla went on to put his money to work in various illicit channels that ranged all the way from hard drugs and prostitution, to extortion, blackmail and high-level political intrigue.

Meanwhile, as his wealth increased, so did his operations. But somehow, even though he maintained residences and power bases in London, Geneva and Rome, he had managed to keep a low profile that earned him a sort of "mystery man" image. He also, according to Duval, was something of a collector, and here, too, the range was wide.

"He is into paintings and antiques," Duval chuckled, "but the story goes that he keeps his cellars stocked with vintage wine, and his bedrooms with beautiful women."

Duval was discreet enough not to ask why I wanted the information on Korla, but he did offer some parting advice.

"Korla is in his late fifties now. That makes him an old lion, *mon ami,* but they are the most dangerous. Be careful, and good luck."

When I hung up I was convinced that handling Korla would be more than just rough. I know the type, with their vicious appetites and their ugly itch for wealth and power. I also felt something else, as though invisible battle lines had been drawn between Korla and myself, making us adversaries even before we met. And so, when I finally approached the floodlit casino glittering high above the curving bay, I found myself looking forward to this meeting with a man I didn't know, but already disliked.

Maitre d's are probably the most unflappable people in the world, and the one at the Casino du Faune ran true to type—that is until I mentioned Korla's name. His response bordered on the miraculous. The guy actually smiled, did a bow from the waist and promptly led me to a reserved table close to the casino's sprawling stage. I refused the menu, and when he suggested I leave the choice of wine to him, I agreed, and off he went.

The Casino du Faune is probably Lebanon's top
tourist draw, a kind of posh Disneyland and Follies
Bergère rolled into one. The decor is black marble,
chrome trim and dazzling crystal that continues right
on into the washrooms; but, like Vegas, the name of
the game is gambling. The floor show is packaged in
France, but the real action centers around the roulette
wheels and dice tables.

When my champagne arrived, an impressive Cliquot
'68, I checked my watch. It was a few minutes past
nine. Korla was already late. Moments later the show
began when a huge transparent ball, to the accompa-
niment of the large band, rose majestically from the
depths below the huge stage. Inside the ball, a little
guy wearing a scarlet suit and a crash helmet drove a
chrome-plated motorcycle around and around the ball
at incredible speed. He got a tremendous round of applause from the crowd, and as the ball descended below the stage, a bevy of eye-stopping showgirls, their
bodies painted gold and silver, were lowered from the
domed ceiling in large crystal cages until they dangled
just above the heads of the cheering customers. It
wasn't great theater, but it was one hell of a show-stop-
per.

The next act involved live elephants and what
seemed to be a herd of performing white stallions. The
crowd loved it, and when the curtain lowered, my
watch read nine-thirty.

I swore under my breath and decided to give Korla
just five more minutes. Suddenly, the maitre d' came
up and whispered close to my ear.

"Would you please come out front, sir? There is
someone waiting with a message."

The "someone" turned out to be a huge man in a
tight-fitting, black chauffeur's uniform. He stood in a
small room off the main lounge, cap in hand. I'm six-
feet-two, and it's rare when I have to look up into a
man's eyes, but this gorilla must have been six-five. He

began to say something, but I couldn't get his dialect and the maitre d' took over.

"He says that he has been sent to bring you to Mr. Korla. There is a car waiting out front."

I didn't like the switch in plans, but I wasn't going to break the meeting off. At the same time, I decided to stick with my own car. I told the maitre d' to tell the big guy that I'd follow him in my car, and after the maitre d' interpreted, the big guy nodded and left. The limo, a hearse-sized black Continental Mark IV with smoke-tinted windows, idled at whisper level alongside a row of clipped hedges that flanked the broad driveway. The huge chauffeur sat behind the wheel, and when one of the parking attendants drove up with my car, the big car eased forward. I climbed into the Mustang and toed the pedal following the limo along the curving driveway, past the gated entranceway and onto the road.

The Mark IV speeded up instantly and I had to bear down hard on the gas to keep up. The night sky was inky dark, almost starless. Clumps of cedar trees bordered the left side of the highway, and occasionally, along open stretches, I caught sight of the sea. I rolled down the driver's window and the scent of blooming honeysuckle and jasmine wafted in. The fragrance reminded me of Hananna, my memory of her tinged with pain. I forced the thought of her from my mind. I had to concentrate on what lay ahead.

About ten minutes later the limo made a right, onto a secondary black-topped road. Some five minutes later I spotted lights flickering through the dense foliage to my right. The car ahead started to slow down, and the brake lights winked red as it began pulling over to the side of the road. I followed right behind, braking to a halt a half-car length behind the limo.

I got out, pocketed the keys, and the chauffeur led the way. The lights I had seen came from a roadside inn, and the outside area that was set up café-style.

The place had a deserted air. A few paper lanterns were strung over the empty outdoor tables, their suffused light scarcely penetrating the surrounding shadows. I heard a movement off to the right, the creak of a chair next to a table set well back under the branches of a large tree.

"Carter!"

I saw his bulk—he was a big, massive man—and he made no attempt to get up when I approached.

He extended his hand. "Janos Korla," he announced flatly.

His grip was moist and soft, like squeezing a blob of unbaked dough. The girl seated beside him was young, with dark hair and the kind of flashy good looks I never confuse with real beauty. I scraped back the chair opposite Korla, sat down and had my first good look at him.

The large fleshy face was expressionless, a bloated mask except for the hooded lids that gave his pale blue eyes a serpentine cast. They stared directly into mine. I waited and he finally hunched forward, his immense pudgy hands clasped together. Gradually, his thick wet lips formed into a loose, rubbery smile.

"My apologies for not meeting you at the Casino," he began in his British-accented English, "but I thought it would be better if we met here. It is far more private, and what we have to say to each other can be said in complete confidence."

I glanced at the girl and Korla chuckled.

"I would introduce you, but Karyn doesn't understand a word of English." He jabbed a meaty thumb in the direction of his chauffeur who was sitting stiffly at a small table near the inn's door. "And neither does my driver." His pudgy hands resumed their clasped position and the rubbery smile returned. "So you see, Mr. Carter, there is no reason for concern. Absolutely none."

I leaned back in my chair. "Good. Then suppose we

take it right from the top. When you called yesterday, you said the Salobin matter was still negotiable. Does that mean you're holding Salobin a prisoner?"

"Let's say he's in my protective custody. There is a difference, you know. But I can assure you he is receiving much better care than he did when Rafai had him."

I nodded. "Then it was your people who broke in, killed Rafai and his men, clubbed me out and then made off with Salobin."

"Precisely," he replied. "But I was within my rights. You see, Mr. Carter, Rafai was originally working for me before he got it into his head to go into business for himself. It was a mistake, and a fatal one at that."

I didn't have to urge him to continue. Apparently, he was quite willing to fill me in on some of the details, at least up to a point. In a casual manner he let me know that he had known about Salobin's disenchantment with his Russian bosses for some time. The information, he claimed, had come to him through a well-placed East German double-agent who had been amply paid for the valuable data. A watch on Salobin was then arranged, and when the elderly missile expert left for the scientific conference to be held in Tiflis, Korla correctly assumed that Salobin would use this opportunity to make his defection to the West complete.

"And everything went beautifully at first," Korla beamed. "When the Russian boarded the train that would take him into Turkey, two of my people were already waiting on the Turkish side. They boarded the train once it had passed through customs, and the rest went like a piece of cake. When the train stopped at Ordu, along the Turkish coast, it was already past nine and was a very dark night. One of my people then got into Salobin's compartment by putting on a porter's white jacket and pretending he had come to make up the Russian's berth. Salobin, in fact, had let him in with no questions asked."

He unclasped his hands and his smile deepened. "The rest was easy. A cloth soaked in chloroform was administered and there was no real struggle. The second man now joined the first, and between them they simply passed Salobin out the compartment window where others were waiting. One of these happened to be Rafai. As I said, it was a dark night, and with the small station practically deserted, it went undetected."

"And that's how Rafai tied in?"

"In a manner of speaking, yes," Korla said and the rubbery lips tightened up. "Actually, I had used Rafai's services on previous occasions and found his work quite satisfactory. Of course, I had paid him well, and his instructions were to deliver Salobin to a place I would rather not say at this time. But the fool decided to bypass me and brought Salobin into Lebanon where he hoped to set up his own arrangement. As you already know, he let word out through certain channels that Salobin was available, which in turn brought you to this part of the world with remarkable speed."

He paused, shifting his bulk to a more comfortable position. "I should say here, however, that your arrival was duly observed. In fact, so was your arrival at the Club Salah, and most of your movements thereafter. Naturally, I could have dealt with Rafai any time I'd choose. I had already learned through sources where he was keeping Salobin, but I preferred to wait. I knew you would insist on having visible proof of Salobin's presence before entering any arrangements, so I simply held off in settling matters with Rafai until you had this proof."

"And now?"

"Well, now that you are convinced that we are dealing with the real Salobin, I am sure that it will be much easier for us to talk business. After all, Mr. Carter, the fact that you weren't killed along with Rafai had nothing to do with compassion. It was important that you remain alive, so that we could have this little chat and hopefully come to an understanding."

I made no attempt to hedge or circle the issue. "How much are you asking for the Russian?"

His pale blue eyes flickered with sudden interest. I had taken him a bit by surprise, but he recovered quickly.

"I like the way you do business," he chuckled. "Frankly, I've always found the French too roundabout, the English boring and the Russians impossible. But Americans are different. So refreshingly frank. So direct—"

"How much?" I repeated.

The hooded lids narrowed and his eyes seemed to lose what little color they had.

"The price for Salobin is five million." He held up one plump hand, the fingers outstretched. "Five million dollars, Carter," he repeated crisply. "It is my one offer. My only offer."

I tried laughing it off. "You're asking ten times Rafai's price. You've got to be kidding. We're poles apart, Korla."

He shook his head. "Not really, and you know it. He pressed his bulk forward and tapped the table thoughtfully. "Consider, if you will, the hard facts. For years your government and the Russians have been sitting down to your SALT talks, discussing arms limitations and détente. But it has been little more than a lot of bluffing on both sides, a kind of floating poker game that has been going on endlessly. While your people have been trying to second guess the Russians, the Russians have been doing the same thing. But if Salobin were made available to your government, the situation could change dramatically.

"Salobin could be the key, the bargaining chip your people need so desperately. Imagine, Carter, what it would mean to your Pentagon chiefs if they knew right this minute precisely where the Russians stand when it comes to, say, multiple warheads. Oh, they know the Russians are into MIRVs, of course, only they don't really know how far. But Salobin knows. He knows that and much more. And I needn't remind you what such hard, factual knowledge would mean; the difference it would make in your government's bargaining position."

He leaned back in his chair and grinned confidently. "In fact, with Salobin on your side, your government would no longer have to play cat-and-mouse with the Russians. They would be in the enviable position of shaping whatever foreign policy they saw fit. And the Russians would have no choice but to tag along, like a puppy at the end of a leash."

Korla's pitch was definitely hard sell, but there was a core of truth in what he said. I had to give him points on that, only I wouldn't admit it. "But there's still no way of knowing what information Salobin really possesses," I countered, "and five million's a lot of green."

"So it is," he shrugged, "but again it is a matter of viewing it in its proper perspective. I recall reading in one of your respected magazines that the cost of running your government comes to one hundred thousand dollars a second in round figures. This means five million dollars would come to about fifty seconds—less than one minute of your government's operating costs." He gave another shrug. "Considering what Salobin has to offer, I'd say your people would be getting a huge bargain."

"Maybe so," I replied matter-of-factly. Frankly, I was ready to start backing off, to stall for time, so I fed him the same story I had given Rafai. "I'll get word back to my people," I went on. "I'll tell them your price and they'll take it from there. That's about all I can do at the moment."

He pumped his head in agreement, then took a

quick glance at his watch. "Are there any further questions?"

There was only one further question. "The girl," I said evenly. "Why did you have her killed?"

For a moment or two he looked genuinely puzzled, but suddenly the pale blue eyes flickered. "Of course. The redhead. The belly dancer who worked at the Club Salah."

"Her name was Hananna," I said very slowly. "She was a lovely girl, and not really mixed up in any of this. But you knew that, Korla, and yet you sent your men in and had her butchered. *Why?*"

He shrugged his shoulders impatiently. "Of course I had her killed, but you should know why better than most. After all, she was Rafai's girl and she had been looking after Salobin. There were things she could have overheard. Things about me. Perhaps she would have kept them to herself, but then she may not. As a professional, Carter, you'll agree that risks aren't allowable in this business. And the girl was a risk." He casually brushed some lint from his sleeve. "I was merely protecting my investment. It was a business decision, pure and simple."

My chair scraped as I jumped to my feet. I grabbed Korla by the lapels, and Karyn let out a little cry of fright. I seldom lose control, but rage swept over me like a tide. I yanked him out of his chair and backhanded him twice across the mouth. Blood spurted from his torn lip. I went for three, and then something solid and heavy punched me between the shoulder blades. I gasped, suddenly remembering the chauffeur.

I dropped Korla and spun around in a low crouch. The big guy's fist lashed out. I ducked and it shot by over my shoulder. I moved inside him, and jabbed a short right into his ribs. He grunted and I hit him again. He gave another grunt, but he managed to bring both fists up and grabbed me at the base of the neck. I reeled as steel bands seemed to close around my throat. I hooked my fingers, jabbing at his eyes, but he had me at arms length and all I clawed was air.

Specks of colored light danced before me. I could barely make out his eyes, which were calm, steady and totally devoid of any emotion. His hands were merely instruments checking the fading strength that ebbed from my body. I tried bunching my neck muscles against the throttling pressure but I was getting nowhere fast.

I tried another tack. I went limp all over, giving him all of my weight to hold. I let my knees buckle, rolled my eyeballs back as far as they could go. The grip around my throat slackened slightly. The message was getting through. I went looser still. I felt his thumbs back off some from my Adam's apple. At the most, I had two or three seconds. I sucked in some air, straightened suddenly and rammed my right knee into his groin.

He let out a howl and his hands flew from my throat. He was in a crouch, clutching his gut, when I chopped the edge of my hand at his throat. He dropped to one knee, but suddenly his hand dipped inside his tunic and a switchblade sprang into view. I kicked out and the tip of my shoe caught him along the underside of his jaw. He dropped like a stone. The silence was monumental when I slowly turned and faced Korla. He sat there calmly, a bloodstained handkerchief pressed to his torn lip.

His tone was mocking. "And now that you've disposed of my chauffeur, Carter, am I next?"

The fight had drained off the rage. I felt emptied, but better for it. "It's your move, Korla. Do we go on from here?"

Slowly, he stuffed the handkerchief into his breast pocket. He managed a cold smile. "Every dog is allowed one bite." Straining, he eased his bulk out of the chair and straightened up. "But remember, Carter, you've already had yours."

I watched while he waddled toward the inn with Karyn tagging behind. At the dimly lit door he turned. "Be prepared to leave Lebanon. The Salobin affair will be concluded elsewhere."

It took me by surprise. "Where?"

"You will be notified."

"When?"

"At the proper time."

A moment later he disappeared inside, the girl at his heels.

The chauffeur was struggling to his knees when I climbed into the Mustang. I hit the ignition, waved and took off. The curving road was dark and deserted, but about ten minutes into the ride, the moon appeared from behind the clouds. I settled back against the seat and relaxed. Hawk would have been furious at my outburst, and he'd have been right. It was inexcusable considering the stakes. It could have caused irreparable damage. What if Korla had broken things off? But he hadn't.

I couldn't help smiling. Like the monkey with his hand in the cookie jar, Korla wouldn't let go to save his hide. He needed me, and his greed was the best insurance I had. But I wasn't conning myself either. Greedy doesn't mean stupid. Far from it. And so far Korla had played a shrewd game. He had not only dealt effectively with Rafai by recovering Salobin, but he had also managed to blow my cover from the very beginning. This had to mean excellent contacts in the right places. The best. No matter how I added it up, the total kept coming out one way. Korla was one smart-ass sonofabitch.

CHAPTER 8

Korla kept his word, or whoever it was speaking for him kept it. The call came through to my room early the following morning and the message was brief. I was to grab a flight the following day for Dubrovnik, a seaport on Yugoslavia's Adriatic coast. When I arrived, I was to register at the Marjoro Hotel where a room would be waiting for me in Korla's name. Additional instructions would follow once I got there.

I tried to spin out the conversation, pick up something, but the guy wasn't buying. He played it like a real dummy. He repeated the name of the hotel, the departure time and hung up. When I replaced the phone, two thoughts spun in my head. One, Salobin had been moved out of Lebanon and was either already in Yugoslavia or was on the way. Two, why Yugoslavia? This was Tito country, a closed society despite its few links with the West, and the last place I'd expect Korla to close his deal. But then I remembered. Yugoslavia was where Korla had been born.

Still, considering his background, I figured he'd be a sure bet for Tito's drop-dead list; but then I'd been around long enough not to expect the expected. I decided this called for two heads, and my call to Hawk was long overdue.

I showered, shaved, dressed and grabbed a quick breakfast in the hotel's coffee shop, then flagged down a cab that took me to the U.S. Consulate's office. This time I had no trouble with the attractive receptionist. Smiling prettily, she got right through to Mr. Baylor. He turned up quickly, led me back down the red-carpeted hallway and, after activating the scrambler phone, courteously disappeared.

The overseas operator had a little trouble, but after a bit I heard the familiar ring of AXE's Washington phone. Della answered, and we said "Hi" and "Goodbye" and she put me through to the old man. By his slurred hello I knew he was chewing the end of one of his foul cigars, and without wasting a second of his valuable time I brought him up to date.

Hawk's impatience can be hair-triggered, provided you're boring him with trivia. But if it's important, he's the most patient listener imaginable. I ran through what had happened, told him about Hananna, my being contacted by Korla, our meeting and the price he had put on turning over Salobin. I also gave him the latest about Yugoslavia. I deliberately left out the part about my belting Korla and my fight with his goon.

"You're lucky," he grunted when I was through.

"How's that?"

"That it's Yugoslavia."

"But don't you find it kind of strange that he should have picked Yugoslavia?"

"Maybe so, but you're still lucky."

Riddles are part of Hawk's style, and I knew better than to interrupt the process. I figured he'd get on with it, and he did.

"Have I ever mentioned Steve Biro, Nick? The partner I worked with back in my OSS days?"

I remembered. Biro and Hawk had worked together with "Wild Bill" Donovan, the head of the Office of Strategic Services, in Switzerland during the final months of World War II, and in a rare reminiscent mood he had once spoken to me about Biro and their war experiences. Some of the conversation started coming back.

"Do I recall your saying, sir, that Biro is directing movies these days?"

"Always has," Hawk snapped back. "Even before the war. And that's where the luck fits in. He's in Yugoslavia right now shooting one of those grade B war flicks, and not far from where you'll be. In fact, Biro does an occasional favor for me just to keep his hand in, and he might be able to help in your dealings with Korla. Biro knows a lot of the local people—World War II partisans who worked with him on some behind-the-line missions during the German occupation. I'd think he and his friends could be of some help. You agree?"

"Very much, sir."

"Good, then take down this number."

I got out my pocket pad and ballpoint pen, and as I jotted down the number where Biro could be reached, Hawk was already moving ahead.

"Now about the ransom, N3, and let's get this straight. You'll stall Korla anyway you see fit, but AXE's policy, as you well know, doesn't include pay-offs. The day we start doing that is the day our effectiveness as an organization is over and done with. What I'm saying, Carter, is that we're not bag men. If it were simply a matter of paying off a blackmailer or a kidnapper, AXE wouldn't have been called in. So you know your mission, and it still holds. Use any trick, in or out of the book, but get Salobin out. And I want it done fast. Sooner, if possible. Are we in agreement on this?"

I gave him a respectful "Yessir," and he came back with one of his usual grunts, then paused thoughtfully. "About that girl, Carter. Hananna. I'm sorry about her. Damn sorry."

"I know, sir," I replied. "And thanks for saying so."

He didn't say goodbye, just a brisk "See you." A moment later the scrambler's amber light came on. We were no longer connected. I hung up just a moment before Baylor reentered the room. He flashed his diplomatic smile.

"Everything satisfactory?"

"Just fine."

Still smiling, he showed me out.

I had another phone call to make, an important one, but it had to be made from a public booth. I turned left a block beyond the Consulate building and crossed the wide boulevard lined with recently constructed high-rise apartment buildings. About three blocks further on, I spotted a telephone kiosk alongside a busy newsstand. I entered and pulled the glass hinged door shut behind me. I fed a coin into the slot and dialed the number of the Middle-East Trading Company. At the third ring the phone was picked up.

"Hello?" The man's voice was distinctly American.

"Hello," I replied. "Is this the stationery department?"

"Yes it is. Who's calling please?"

"Section fifty. I've run out of order blanks and I'll need about five thousand more in a hurry, plus a new set of folders. Delivery has to be some time this evening."

I heard him swallow. "The order blanks are no problem, but I can't promise on the folders. It's just that we're a bit short-handed these days."

What the AXE field representative was saying was that the five thousand dollars posed no difficulties, but that the same didn't hold true for a new passport with a fresh cover. But the fact that Korla had blown my present cover made it essential that I have a new set of traveling papers before departing for Yugoslavia. AXE, like any other world-wide organization, isn't free of personnel or logistic problems, but I wasn't going to take no for an answer—not even a maybe.

"Delivery has to be this evening," I repeated, "and I damn well mean a complete delivery. So get the lead out."

The snarl in my voice got him moving.

"Can do," he said briskly. "I'll just have to reshuffle some of the priorities."

I gave him the name of my hotel and my present cover name. "This evening," I repeated.

When he reaffirmed it, I gave him a firm thank you and hung up.

When I left the phone booth I spotted a movie house across the street that was playing "The Godfather." Since I had a few hours to kill before getting back to the hotel, I bought a ticket and went in. There was a dubbed sound track and listening to Brando mumbling away in Arabic kept me chuckling most of the way. When the film ended and the lights came on, I got a few rough stares from the people around me. I ducked out while the crowd showed its appreciation by applauding the blank screen—a custom throughout the Mid-East.

By my watch it was a little past four and as my eyes swept the flow of traffic, looking for a cab, some instinct pulled my head around. The man was off to my left. He stood close to the edge of the curb, a newspaper rolled up and tucked under his right arm. He was on the tall side, slim, his eyes masked by a pair of green-tinted, metal-rimmed shades. He seemed to give me a quick glance, then let his gaze drift over the passing traffic. Like myself, he could have been looking for a cab, but my radar was flashing signals. I turned, pushing my way through the crowd that was emptying from the theater.

At the corner a bus waited for the light to change, its door open. I had no idea where the bus was going, but at the moment this was small potatoes. I dropped some coins into the fare box, and just as the doors started to close, the guy with the shades barged in. I dropped into a seat near the center doors, and when he came down the aisle the bus started up and he grabbed the overhead handrail. Gradually, he worked his way back, clutching the rail, and ignoring a couple of empty seats. He showed me his back and unrolled his paper.

The next stop was a busy one. A steady stream came aboard and, as they shuffled to the rear, my view of him was temporarily blocked. A moment later a large woman, her flabby arms loaded with packages, stepped down and the center doors popped open. I followed right out behind her, heard the doors snap shut. Black smoke belched from the exhaust as the bus took off.

I flagged down a passing cab, hopped in and gave the driver the name of my hotel. My feelings were mixed. He could've been a tail, but I couldn't be sure.

When I arrived at the hotel I checked with the desk before going to my room. Before leaving to call Hawk, I had told the clerk to book me on the morning flight to Dubrovnik, and he told me that everything was in order. I thanked him, told him to have my bill ready in the morning and to be on the lookout for a package arriving in my name.

"Shall I send it up, sir?"

I told him to do that, and headed for the elevators.

About an hour later—much earlier than I had anticipated—the uniformed messenger arrived with AXE's package. I signed the slip, tipped him and reclosed the door. I thumbed the brown wrapper open and dumped the contents on the bed. AXE's money is almost always new. The crisp fifties were in packets of twenty, five in all. I checked the new passport. It carried the official Lebanon visa stamp and it was made out in the name of Howard Kierzek. Since my destination was Yugoslavia, whoever came up with the new cover name probably figured that Kierzek had a good ethnic ring. Getting out my old passport, I removed the photograph of myself and pasted it into the new one. I then transferred the money into another envelope, signed and sealed it. Shortly afterward I took the elevator down.

On the way out I stopped at the desk, handed the envelope to the clerk and told him to put it in the safe. When I had pushed my way through the revolving doors, a cabbie spotted me and eased over to the curb. I climbed in, pulling the door shut behind me. His head swiveled in my direction.

"The Emporium. Rue Galland."

He pumped his head, let the clutch fly.

The Emporium is probably one of the best restaurants in Beirut, a reminder of the old days when the French administered Lebanon. The service is still first class, white-gloved in fact, but I was in a self-indulgent mood. I ached every time I thought of Hananna. She would have loved the place.

I ordered sweetbreads, the house salad, a fillet of sole veronique and a half-bottle of vintage Chablis. It was perfection throughout, including the basket of warm rolls. I ate leisurely, dawdled in fact. By the time the demitasse arrived, two hours had slipped by. The tab, plus the service charge, came to a little more than twelve pounds, about thirty American taxpayers' dollars. I had indulged all right, but there wasn't the slightest twinge of guilt.

When I left the restaurant I decided to walk back to my hotel. The night was humid, full of pungent odors that drifted out of dark, narrow streets and even darker alleys. I stopped at the corner, waited for a break in the traffic, and then I spotted him again—the guy with the shades. He stood by a newsstand, clutching an opened magazine, but enough of his profile showed for me to recognize him.

I don't place too much faith in the long arm of coincidence. When I can spot the same face within hours in a city of more than half-a-million, I start playing it close to the chest.

When the traffic broke I stepped right out. I crossed with the crowd, but through the corner of my eye I saw him move. He fell in behind, but maintained a cautious distance. Someone had assigned me a baby-sitter, no doubt about it. It hit me that he could be one of Korla's men, but for the moment that wasn't important. Right now I had to shake him.

When I reached the other side of the street, I deliberately slowed down. It's an old trick when dealing with a tail, but an effective one. What it does is force the tail's hand. Rather than slow down with you, which could be a give away, they'll generally pass you and then double back to your rear. Anyway, the ploy worked. While I continued to slow down, he suddenly picked up speed and swept right past me, eyes straight ahead. Moments later I spotted the dark, narrow alley to my right. It was tailor-made. I ducked in, felt rough cobblestones underfoot. Faint light showed at the far end. I made my way carefully, staying close to the shadowy walls of the dark, silent buildings.

About half way through I stepped up my pace. By now, I thought I had definitely pried him loose, when I suddenly heard the rapid footsteps. They came from ahead and to the left. A second later I spotted the alley that fed directly into the one I was in. The approaching footsteps picked up speed. Obviously, he had noted my disappearance and had taken the next alley and was now backtracking in my direction. I flattened against the wall as he burst into view.

He glanced both ways, hesitated. I stepped back, to make better use of the shadows and my heel struck a pile of garbage. Bottles and cans clattered. His hand came up. I dove, heard the muffled *thowwkk* of the silencer, like a cork popping. I rolled as I hit the ground. There was another *thowwkk*. Sparks flew from the cobblestones alongside my head as I came up with Wilhelmina. I was on my belly when I snapped off my first shot, the roar shattering the silence. My second shot was in. He spun drunkenly, his hands clutching his throat. He dropped face down.

The bullet had torn open his throat, severing his jugular, and he was probably dead by the time I reached him; or would be soon. There was no time for a search. Windows began popping open and lights flared on. Shouts began to break out. I swept up his fallen gun, dropped it into my pocket and took off. The one thing I didn't need was to be picked up by the local fuzz.

I pounded through the alley, but broke into a walk just before coming out the far side into a wide street. I blended into the crowd, and two blocks further on I picked up a cab. I gave the driver the name of my hotel and instructed him to drop me off at the side entrance. Ten minutes later we arrived and I took the service elevator to my floor. Once I was in my room, with the door locked, I got out the gun.

It was a Ruger .41 single-action revolver with a four-and-a-half-inch barrel. I unscrewed the mounted silencer and checked the remaining bullets. They were soft-nosed, the kind that mushrooms on contact. It's the preferred choice of professional assassins since they can rip a hole in a victim's body the size of a billiard ball.

I used a few sheets of newspaper to wrap the gun and after tying the bundle securely I rang room service. I really needed a drink. When it arrived, I tipped the bellhop, relocked the door and settled back.

I sipped at the scotch slowly and thoughtfully.

Whoever had dispatched the hatchet man would be disappointed. But where there had been one there could be others. There was no way my getting around it. Obviously, someone wanted me dead in a very bad way.

CHAPTER 9

At eighteen thousand feet the Adriatic looked like a shimmering blue scarf beneath a thin layer of scattered clouds. We were about two-and-a-half hours into our flight and the two pretty Yugoslavian stewardesses moved briskly down the aisle, gathering up the last of the coffee cups and stacking them on plastic trays. I glanced at my watch. It was about twenty minutes to touchdown. So far the flight had been strictly routine.

During the drive to Beirut's international airport that morning, I turned frequently to look out the cab's rear window, but saw nothing to make me suspicious that I had picked up another tail. Before boarding the JAT DC-3 for Dubrovnik I had managed to get rid of the wrapped silencer by dropping it into one of the airport's litter baskets. Once aboard, I scanned my fellow passengers and they looked fairly typical: some businessmen carrying attaché cases, a few families and a clutch of German tourists.

After takeoff I settled back and relaxed, at least up

to a point. Right then I was fairly certain that whoever had tried to nail me in the alley the night before hadn't been put up to it by Korla. It simply didn't wash. Korla wanted his five million in a bad way, and without me he'd be out of the money. So if it wasn't Korla, then *who?*

Like most questions, it raised interesting speculations. Of course, the Russians couldn't be ruled out. By now they'd be pretty determined to locate Salobin, and if they had gotten on to Korla, and tied me in with him, it figured they could've sent one of their hired guns after me. But there were other possibilities.

For example, Korla may have fed me a pack of lies. Maybe Rafai had never worked for him. And if Rafai had been tied in with someone else, and Korla got wind of it, he may have simply muscled in on the hope of collecting big. In fact, at this point I couldn't even be sure he had Salobin. The hit man who took my bullet in his throat could have been a member of a rival faction after the same prize. Likely? Maybe. But I couldn't be sure.

I was still kicking these and other possibilities back and forth when the DC-3 began its descent. We bumped and shook as vaporous clouds swept past the wingtips. Banking slowly, the plane swung into its final landing pattern. There was a noticeable drag as the flaps came down, and a solid bump when the landing gear locked in. The pitch of the engines shifted, becoming a piercing whine. As we dropped lower, the view of the coastline through the window sharpened noticeably. Tiny black spots peppered the curving beach. People. Sunlight glinted across slanted rooftops. Beyond the sprawling city, row after row of snow-capped mountains receded to the horizon.

Minutes later we touched down and bounced fairly hard. The brakes hissed and grabbed, cutting the speed way down. When we gently taxied off the runway and turned onto the concrete apron, the Germans lunged to their feet. Shouting and shoving, they were the first ones off.

After passing through customs I went to the airport's currency exchange desk and had AXE's dollars converted into *dinars*. I speak enough Serbo-Croatian to get by, and I had no trouble getting through to the cabbie who took me to the Marjoro, the hotel where Korla had reserved a room. It was on the fourth floor, and the wide window looked out on the beach and the sparkling sea.

I had showered, and was thinking about lunch, when the phone rang. I recognized Korla's voice instantly and he didn't waste a second. There were going to be a few delays, was the way he phrased it, but he assured me that everything was going according to plan and that he'd be getting back to me very soon.

"How soon?" I demanded.

I had put a deliberate edge in my voice and he quickly sensed it.

"I don't know," he replied testily. "You will just have to wait and see. It could be two or three days before we get straightened out on this end." He paused. "Are you becoming restless, Mr. Carter?"

I had him going in the right direction. "Not restless, but I don't intend to hang on to the end of this phone for the next seventy-two hours or more. If you need the time, fine, but don't handcuff me to your schedule."

There was another pause, a longer one, but when he spoke again there was more of a conciliatory tone to his voice. "Agreed, but if you're going to be gone for any length of time, leave word where you can be reached."

I promised I would, and hung up before he could click off. I believed that Korla was leveling. There was a good chance that Salobin may have still been enroute from wherever they had been keeping him. It also figured that Korla may have wanted the time to check me out, to make certain I hadn't set him up for some kind of counterplot. Meanwhile, my tough approach on the phone had worked. In effect, it put Korla on notice that I wouldn't take any crap he might try to hand out, plus the fact that I wasn't going to babysit the telephone while waiting for his call. In fact, with the next few days being open, I figured it was as good a time as any to get in touch with Steve Biro, Hawk's wartime buddy from the OSS.

Getting out my memo pad with Biro's number, I dialed the desk. Biro was on location below Kotor, making it a long distance call. There was a brief wait, and then the clerk came back on. He apologized for the delay, but the lines to Kotor were tied up temporarily.

"*Hitno je?*"

He wanted to know if it was very urgent. I told him it wasn't and that I'd be coming downstairs. When the call came through he could page me in the bar. He said he would, thanked me, and buzzed off.

The bar was just about deserted when I got there. It was off the lobby, and the bartender, a balding, round-faced man, flashed a friendly, gold-toothed smile. I ordered a small glass of *rakija,* a kind of one-gulp plum brandy that goes down like liquid fire. When I set the empty glass down, he was back with the bottle.

"*Jos jednu?*" Another round?

I nodded, and he refilled it to the brim. This time I didn't gulp. I treated it with the respect it deserved, sipping at it slowly. The bartender busied himself, polishing his glassware with a small towel. The minutes ticked by. Suddenly a phone rang. It was behind the bar, at my end. The bartender picked it up, spoke briefly, then looked at me and asked if I were Howard Kierzek. My call had come through. I took the instrument from his outstretched hand.

"Hello. Mr. Biro?"

"Who's this?" It was a booming voice, commanding but still friendly.

I didn't bother with my cover name. I simply said that I was an overseas representative of the "Amalgamated Press and Wire Services" and he made the AXE connection instantly. The voice boomed on. He said he had received a call from the "old man" in Washington only the day before, alerting him that I'd be getting in touch. Without a pause he invited me to come on down.

"How soon can you leave?"

"This afternoon would be fine, providing that's okay with you."

"Great," he boomed back. "We've had to stop shooting this morning. Some sound equipment problems. But that'll give us a chance to talk. Always wanted to meet you, in fact."

I got out my pad and began writing the instructions he gave me for the drive down.

"The trip shouldn't take you more than a couple of hours," he concluded. "It's a beautiful drive, some of the nicest scenery in Yugo."

I thanked him again and started to say goodbye, when he suddenly interrupted.

"You like bourbon?"

"Love it."

"Great," he bellowed. "We're gonna get along just fine."

After a quick lunch in the hotel's restaurant I had the desk phone for a car rental. There were a couple of choices, but I figured I'd save the taxpayers some money and settled for a Fiat. The car agency said they'd have someone drive it over and it arrived within a half-hour, a bright red little job and spanking clean. Minutes later I drove off. My one piece of luggage was in the trunk. I don't like leaving luggage in an empty hotel room if I can avoid it.

Biro and his crew were on location about midpoint between Kotor and Budva, but the road is circuitous since it loops around the Bay of Kotor, making it a

longer trip than the actual miles involved. Once Dubrovnik was behind me, the highway hugged the picturesque coastline and I passed beach after beach that
makes this part of the Adriatic such a great tourist
draw. But about a half hour later the countryside
changed abruptly. It became wilder, rougher. The
beaches disappeared, replaced by rock strewn shoreline. Road traffic also fell off noticeably. I stopped once
to check my direction at a small fishing village, then
swung back onto the main road. It wasn't much later
when I spotted the car coming up behind in my rearview mirror. For a second or two I thought he wanted
to pass, but when I eased over, gave him the road, he
cut back on his speed and maintained a steady distance
in between.

Automatically, the warning flags began popping up.
From what I could see through the mirror, the car
looked like a Porsche, but I wasn't too sure. For a while
we played the old footsie game. When I'd toe down on
the gas, spurt ahead, he moved up fast to close the
widening gap. But when I'd ease off, he followed suit
immediately. An idiot couldn't miss the telltale signs. I
had picked up another tail.

I figured it might be one of Korla's boys sent out to
keep an eye on me, but I couldn't be sure. There was a
second possibility. After the shoot-out the night before
in Beirut, there was a good chance that another hit
man had been dispatched.

While I mulled this dark possibility over, the road
ahead curved sharply. I banked into it, and when I
came out of it a road sign flashed by. A village was up
ahead. I came down on the pedal and the Fiat moved
out. Reaching inside my jacket, I withdrew Wilhelmina
from my shoulder holster and wedged the small luger's
barrel under my right thigh. I wasn't out to buy
trouble, but I wasn't taking any unnecessary chances.
Meanwhile, the up-coming village was a piece of luck.

Once I got there the cat-and-mouse game could be broken off.

I continued to come down on the gas pedal and the speedometer needle swung right, began edging past the 75 line. From behind came the roar of the oncoming car. I rechecked the rear mirror. He was well over to the left, out of the curve, moving very fast. Obviously, he had spotted the village sign and had decided to make his move before we'd get there.

I floored the pedal as the distance between us shrunk, but the spunky little Fiat was no match. Swiftly, the distance closed. In a few seconds he'd be alongside. The road was arrow straight, flanked on the left by a thick wall of rushing pines, and with the sea on my right. I gauged the width of the road's right shoulder. It was mostly sand, powdery, with tufts of sprouting grass. I swerved onto it, the steering wheel jerking viciously as I left the road. I backed off on the gas, fought the wheel. I gave the brakes two light taps. The Fiat's rear fishtailed right-left, the spinning tires throwing a cloud of sand and flying grass as he swept by.

I wasn't much of a target, but I heard the two shots; the double ping of metal. Pumping the Fiat's brakes, I cut left, swinging back onto the tarmac. By the time I came to a skidding halt, the Porsche was a black speck fleeing towards infinity.

I took a couple of quick breaths, tucked Wilhelmina back inside my shoulder holster and stepped outside to have a look. Considering the haze he had fired through, he hadn't done too badly. One of the bullets had nicked the chrome just above the driver's window, and the second had grooved a two-inch metal scar on the roof. It was close. I got out my handkerchief, dusted the sand from the Fiat's windshield and climbed back in.

The remainder of the trip was anti-climactic. At Zelenika, a small port village, I turned left and followed the road that circled the unruffled bay. About ten minutes later I drove into Perast, got a few more directions, and twenty or so minutes later I arrived in Kotor. I had no trouble getting a line on Biro's movie set. A tall, white-gloved policeman in the town's main square patiently heard me through, and when I made some movements with my hands, to indicate movie cameras at work, he caught on even faster.

Grinning, he pointed straight ahead. *"Pravo. Pazi na vos. Skrenite levo. Pravo, pravo."*

I was to go straight on to the railroad crossing, then make a left turn. From here it would be straight all the way.

I thanked him, and as I took off he threw me a brisk salute.

It took less than five minutes to get to the railroad crossing, and I swung left as instructed. The dirt-topped road was narrow and rutted, and the Fiat's springs groaned painfully. Five minutes later the road tilted upward and I had to shift into low. About thirty or so yards later I topped the steep rise, but I was in no way prepared for the incredible sight below. Stretching out in all directions was a battlefield mock-up that looked like something straight out of World War II.

Barbed wire and the burnt-out hulks of German tanks dotted a huge, lumpy field that had been torn up and cratered to give the effect of repeated shelling. Biro's prop men had certainly done a bang-up job. They had even blasted off the limbs of some of the few remaining trees, and they looked like the old wartime pictures published years ago in *Life* and *Time*.

Impressed, I released the footbrake and began inching my way down. Movie extras wearing German uniforms and ragged partisan battle jackets milled all over the place. It must have been break time because they were lolling around, eating from paper bags and sipping coffee from plastic cups. I pulled up alongside one group perched atop a gutted German ammo carrier with a swastika emblazoned on the engine hood.

"Anyone here speak English?"

A tall guy with a crew cut, and wearing an S.S. Sturmbannfuhrer's uniform, hopped down and came over. If he weren't munching a candy bar I would have expected him to yell "Achtung!" but he said "Hi" in a soft British accent, smiled agreeably, and politely waited for me to take it from there.

"I'm looking for Steve Biro. "Do you know where I can find him?"

"No problem," he assured me, and pointed to a stand of birch trees at the far end of the scarred field. "Mr. Biro's trailer is behind those trees. He may be wandering around the set, but if you see his Mercedes he's probably there."

I thanked him, and he waved goodbye, heading back to his friends.

Lurching and bouncing, I cut across the field toward the birches. When I cut around them I spotted the trailer with a black Mercedes parked alongside. I pulled up behind, gave the Fiat's horn two light bleeps and got out. When I slammed the door behind me, the trailer door popped open and a large-boned man in his late fifties filled the narrow doorway. I immediately recognized the craggy face topped with its mop of iron grey hair from his pictures in the news weeklies. He put out a big knuckled hand and practically pulled me into the trailer.

"Carter, this is one hell of a pleasure," he boomed. "I mean that. Hawk tells me you're the best, and that's enough for me."

The fact that Hawk would have said something like that was both surprising and flattering, and while I thanked Biro for inviting me down he waved to a chair. "Forget it," he grinned. "And now for some bourbon."

The trailer was littered with books and magazines, and mountains of paper were piled everywhere. But he knew his way around. After poking into a corner, he came up with a couple of paper cups and set them on the narrow table between us. From a wall cupboard came an unopened bottle of Old Crow. He slit the government sticker with his thumbnail and set the bottle down. The small refrigerator provided a tub of cubes and a siphon of soda water. He dropped two cubes into each cup, splashed in a generous amount of the Old Crow.

He patted the siphon. "Need any?"

I shook my head.

He nodded approval and raised his cup. "Cheers."

He drank noisely, his big Adam's apple bobbing up and down. Settling back, he replenished his drink and pushed the bottle my way. "So let's get down to business," he grinned. "From the little Hawk told me, it seems you're after a pretty big fish and I want you to know right off, Nick, that I'll do all I can to help. But remember, I don't have to be told everything—just what you think I ought to know and skip the rest. Fair enough?"

I appreciated his frankness, and during the next few minutes I filled him in on what I thought necessary. I didn't mention Salobin by name, but only said that he was a Russian missile expert who had defected, was in turn kidnapped, and that he was due to arrive in Yugoslavia shortly. I told him about Korla, of course, that he had apparently masterminded the snatch, and that my express mission was to get the kidnapped Russian out of the country and into American hands.

I didn't spell out precisely why Salobin was that important—though Biro probably guessed—and other than mentioning my original meeting with Korla in Beirut, I left out the part about Hananna and the two attempts that had been made on my life. I also made no mention of the ransom figure.

"What I'm looking for right at this moment," I concluded, "is a line on Korla's whereabouts. And this is where Hawk thought you and your Yugoslavian contacts could be of help. I'm assuming Korla is in the country because he called me at my hotel only this morning, and it would be a big help to me if I could pinpoint his whereabouts."

Biro drained his cup, chuckled. "It could be I'm a little ahead of you, Nick. When Hawk called to tell me you might be dropping by, he also told me about Korla, and asked me to do some preliminary checking. And I did. I made inquiries through some of my old partisan buddies who are on the receiving end of some pretty good underground pipelines. They say Korla is a first rate bastard, but that's something you already know. But they also told me that he has a spacious apartment in Belgrade where he stays once or twice a year, plus a seaside villa below Dubrovnik. It's a renovated eighteenth-century castle. If he's in the country at the present time there's a good chance he'd be in one of these two places. Which one I can't say right now, but my friends are working on it and I may know soon."

Biro was already proving helpful, and that led to a question that had been bugging me for the past two days.

"But how is it," I asked, "that a guy with Korla's background could have this kind of entree in Yugoslavia? After all, this is an iron-curtain country, and I'd imagine a wheeler-dealer like Korla would have been given the boot a long time back."

Biro chuckled again. "Right. But then Tito's brand of communism isn't anything like the Moscow or Mao variety. If this were, say, Roumania or Albania, the likes of Korla wouldn't get a foothold. But I repeat, Yugoslavia is different and you'd better believe it."

Still chuckling, he replenished my drink and then his own. "Just ask any Yugoslavian," he continued, "what kind of government he's living under and he'll promptly say, 'Communist.' But what other Communist government has advertising, profit sharing, black markets and some of the slickest call girls in the business to keep the tourists happy? And then there's their relaxed life style that you just don't find in any other Communist country. Take their famous skinny-dipping beaches, for example. Hell, between Kotor and Dubrovnik alone you can see more bare ass and boobs than you will in Southern California *or* the French Riveria!"

"I'll buy that," I smiled. "Yugoslavia doesn't fit the Communist mold, but does that really explain Korla's presence?"

He shrugged, swirling the bourbon around in his cup. "Maybe not precisely, Nick, but it sort of all hangs together when you consider Korla's background. Now you know that the guy was born here and that he dealt in black market penicillin during the war—and that's an important clue. If you remember your World War II history, you'll recall that when the Germans invaded Yugoslavia in 1941, the resistance forces were headed up by Draja Mikhailovich, a Chetnik. But two years later, Tito and his Communist partisans were able to boot Mikhailovich out and they took over the entire partisan movement.

"There's a connection here, and according to my knowledgeable old buddies, Korla got into the act somewhere around this time. I guess Tito looked like a winner to Korla, because my friends say that's when Korla began to supply Tito's rag-tag army with penicillin and other vital medical material that was in very short supply. Still, this doesn't mean that Korla was giving it away for free. After all, Tito was being funded by the British as well as the United States, and Korla was getting cash on the barrelhead for every drop he made. Maybe Korla was shrewdly looking down the road a bit. He knew the war would have to come to an end someday, and he probably figured making powerful friends in the right places wouldn't hurt in the least."

The picture began to emerge. "Then you're saying that Korla bought his way into the new movement."

Biro shrugged and ran thick fingers through his bushy hair. "Not exactly, Nick. But I am suggesting that Korla proved himself to be useful to the struggling new forces, and I'd say it was good survival thinking on their part to use whatever help they could get. Naturally, savory tidbits like these don't get into the history books, but my sources of information say that Korla continued to assist the new government by providing a variety of scarce commodities even after the war was over. And the fact that Korla was known as a man who dealt from the bottom of the deck didn't matter."

Biro shook his head wearily. "The end of the war did more than just change the map of Europe. Along with the new governments came new people. All the old alliances were falling apart and new ones were being shaped in the back rooms. A lot of horse trading was going on. And I'm sure that Korla had a hand in it. In fact, I'm sure he's still got a hand in many of the black market operations that are flourishing inside Yugoslavia right at this moment. That's why he can feel reasonably secure here. Obviously, because he feels secure, there must be people in high authority who are looking the other way when Korla wheels and deals."

He picked up the bottle of bourbon and held it to the light. It was half-gone anyway. "The trouble with this stuff," he laughed, "is that it puts a knot in your gut while it loosens your tongue. Here I am handing you a lot of academic crap, when all you really want and need is some solid information to put you on Korla's trail. Ain't that the truth, Nick?"

In a way it was, but what he had said impressed me and I was about to tell him so when there was a light knock on the trailer's door. When Biro opened it I couldn't see the girl because his back blocked the view, but I heard her voice. It was low-keyed, on the husky side—the English fluent but lightly accented. Biro said something about 'checking into it' and then suddenly he was inviting her in.

"Maya," he boomed, "I want you to meet one hell of a nice guy."

Maya was a total surprise. She was about twenty-five, dark-haired and on the tall side. The fact that she wore jeans and a man-tailored shirt in no way detracted from her stunning figure. She came forward, smiling, and her eyes put a catch in my throat—large and luminous, they were a shade of purest violet.

Biro stood behind her, obviously grinning at my startled expression. "This is Maya Hanash," he beamed. "My script girl, and the best one I ever had."

Since Biro didn't know my cover name, I quickly took over. "Howard Kierzak," I said, taking her hand. I shot Biro a quick glance. "Mr. Biro and I have a mutual old friend who insisted that we get together if I got to Yugoslavia. Now that I'm meeting you, the trip has become even more pleasurable."

She laughed easily, and then her expression suddenly turned thoughtful. "Kierzak," she murmured. "Isn't that a Croatian name?"

"My grandfather's," I lied, and I hated doing it. "He came to the United States after World War I and settled in Ohio. But that was a long time ago."

Biro tactfully broke in. "I hate to interrupt you two, but Maya tells me that the sound equipment that broke down this morning is ready to roll, so I'll have to get cracking. But I've got an idea. Why don't the three of us have dinner tonight?"

For a moment I hesitated. It occurred to me that Korla might try to reach me, and that I should be getting back to Dubrovnik. But Biro persisted.

"You ask him, Maya."

"Please?" she smiled, her hand on my arm.

"Okay," I agreed. It was all the coaxing I needed.

Biro stepped outside with her, but a moment later he was back, closed the door behind him. "Beautiful, isn't she?" he grinned.

"Absolutely stunning."

He chuckled and filled me in on some of her background. "Lost her parents when she was a kid, and was raised by an uncle who sent her to Switzerland for her schooling. Besides English, she speaks French, all the Yugoslavian dialects, and some German as well. In an operation like this, language can be a problem. I've got a polyglot cast. My leading actress is Italian and my male lead is French. The atmosphere people are Greeks, Yugoslavians, Germans, Czechs and God knows what else. It doesn't make for good communication, and I'd be a dead loss without that girl. When the going gets tough I just yell, 'Maya!' and she'll pop up at my elbow and sort out the confusion in no time."

He paused, his bushy brows puckered in thought. "Ordinarily," he said slowly, "I don't interfere in things like this. In fact, Nick, my leading lady would screw her ass off for a big, good-looking guy like you and it wouldn't bother me in the least." He stopped for another pause. "But Maya's something else," he went on. "She's a kind of private person, sensitive—" He broke off and dropped an arm around my shoulder. "I just thought it was something I ought to say. You're not put off because I brought it up?"

I shook my head. "Not in the least, Steve. I'm glad you did." And I meant it.

He walked me out to the car, and when I slid in behind the wheel of the Fiat he gave me directions to the hotel he was staying at in Kotor, the Fjord, where we'd be having dinner and where I'd be able to book a room. I started up the Fiat, and suddenly a dull boom pounded the air. Two more followed right behind. Puffs of black smoke drifted over the tops of some shattered trees.

"They're warming up for the artillery scene," Biro explained. "I'd better go look."

When he loped off, I put the car in gear and moved out. Some of the tanks had started to roll, and groups of extras in infantry uniforms were bunched up behind. Flat trucks with camera crews had taken their positions alongside and some smoke machines were working along the edges of the field. As the heavy guns continued to pound away, some light machinegun fire began chattering away. I drove to the top of the steep hill and stopped for another look. More artillery had joined in, and along with the lumbering tanks and advancing infantry, it began to look like World War II all over again. I released the brake and started down. From behind, the make-believe guns of war rumbled on. At the bottom of the hill I turned left in the direction of Kotor.

The Fjord Hotel faces the bay and has its own private beach and swimming pool. The brouchure I picked up in the lobby claimed 250 rooms, all of them equipped with private baths and their own balcony. I got a corner room on the second floor that offered a view of the sea from one window and soaring Mt. Lovćen from the other.

One of the first things I did was to call the Marjoro Hotel in Dubrovnik. The desk clerk had received no calls for me, and I went on to tell him that I could be away for a day or two and that he was to tell any caller that I could be reached at the Fjord. I had him take down the number, thanked him and hung up.

It was getting on to six now, which left about an hour before Biro and Maya would arrive. I showered and shaved, then had room service send up a drink. Between sips I puffed at a cigarette and glanced through some magazines, but my thoughts kept going back to Maya. I've known a lot of beautiful women in my time, but Maya had that rare extra something that defies description. I suppose the word for it is charisma, but that doesn't quite say it. We had only met for a few minutes, spoken briefly, but a kind of inexplicable magic had taken place all the same. I tried applying the brakes.

Easy, Nick, I said to myself. Keep this up and you'll start climbing the walls.

I went back to the magazines, but Maya's intriguing violet eyes kept floating between myself and the pages. Suddenly the phone shrilled. It was the desk, calling to say that Biro and Maya were waiting downstairs. I took the stairway down, two steps at a time, then pulled up short.

"Cool it, Nick," I muttered. "You're acting like a seventeen-year-old."

She was seated in the lobby, her long legs neatly crossed. She was on her feet the moment she saw me. She had changed into a dark skirt with a small floral print and a long-sleeved white satin blouse that buttoned at the wrists. Her dark, flowing hair was brushed to a glowing sheen, and she looked even lovelier than when we had met that afternoon. Biro wasn't with her, but she quickly explained.

"He's in the bar making a few calls, but he said we should go right in and get a table and to be sure and order him a double scotch."

The dining room was large, but we found a comfortable corner booth. I ordered double scotches for Biro and me, and the sherry Maya requested. After the drinks arrived we settled back and chatted. I asked how she liked her job and she said it never stopped being exciting. We also talked about her schooling in Switzerland, and then she asked me what I did. I told her I was a sales rep for a Grand Rapids furniture

company, and that I was principally in the country on
business. I kept the details on the vague side, ex-
plaining I was looking to buy up quantities of furniture
in the raw that could be finished in our domestic
plants. Her eyes sparkled with interest. Besides everything else, she was a great listener.

It was about here that Biro showed up. Slumping in
his seat, he finished off his drink in two neat gulps and
immediately ordered another.

"Better let Maya order," he suggested. "That way
we can't go wrong."

The meal was excellent. We started out with a thick,
meaty soup, and then Maya suggested I try a *culbastija*
that turned out to be one of the best steaks I had ever
eaten. I had two bowls of salad, rolls and a variety of
vegetables. I skipped dessert, but finished off with two
cups of *turska kava,* a Turkish coffee that can blitz a
Saturday night hangover in thirty seconds flat.

Not long after the table was cleared, Biro swung to
his feet. At this point the conversation had become
mostly two-sided, between Maya and me, and Biro
wasn't slow about catching on.

"Don't either of you try to stop me," he grinned,
"but I'll just shove off to the bar."

Maya watched him go, smiling fondly. "He's been
like a father to me. A wonderful, wonderful person."

I very much wanted to make a long night of it, but it
wasn't too long after Biro left that Maya glanced at her
watch. "We begin shooting very early tomorrow morning," she apologized. "I'm afraid I'll have to be getting
back."

I was disappointed, but I insisted on driving her
home. I asked for the check, but the waiter told me
that Biro had left word that it be put on his bill. I left
a tip, brought Maya out to the lobby and then went to
see Biro in the bar. I told him I'd be taking Maya
home, and then he explained about his pre-dinner calls.

"They were to some of my old partisan friends," he said in a lowered tone, "and they promised to get right on it. I think they'll be able to get a line on Korla's whereabouts fairly soon. At the most a couple of days, but it could even be sooner."

I thanked him again, picked Maya up in the lobby, and we went out to the lot where I had parked the Fiat. It was a beautiful evening, with a light westerly breeze blowing in across the bay. Maya pointed out the way. She rented a small cottage on the outskirts of town, and it took under twenty minutes to get there. I parked alongside what looked like a garden wall, and after we got out we walked up the short bordered path to the front door.

She removed the key from her purse and paused. I kissed her gently, on the cheek. She returned it, hesitated for a moment, and then placed her mouth over mine. Her arms slid around my neck. It was totally unexpected. Her arms tightened, and suddenly a phone inside the house started to ring. Her lips withdrew and she gave a low laugh. The phone kept going. I counted the rings: five . . . six . . . seven . . .

She laughed again. "I'm afraid it won't stop. Perhaps I'd better—"

Eight . . . nine . . .

"What about tomorrow, Maya?"

"I'd like that," she replied. "I'll call from location. The very first chance."

She slipped the key in the lock, flashed another smile. A moment later she stepped inside and the door closed silently behind her.

I waited until the phone stopped ringing, then returned to the car. When I got back to the hotel I stopped at the bar, but Biro had left, so I went directly to my room. When I was in bed and had switched off the lamp, I found myself wondering who Maya's caller could have been. I felt it had to be a man, and I experienced a quick stab of honest-to-goodness jealousy. I closed my eyes.

"Carter," I thought aloud sleepily, "what you need is a good swift kick in the butt."

CHAPTER 10

It was a bit past noon and I was sprawled out beside the hotel pool when my name boomed over the intercom. There was a phone call waiting for me in the lobby. I slipped into my robe and a pair of canvas slippers and padded over. When the clerk spotted me, he held up two fingers and pointed to a row of phones that stood on a marble shelf. I picked up number two and said hello.

Maya's voice came through instantly. She sounded breathless and excited. The day's shooting had gone very well and she expected they'd wrap up work by four that afternoon.

"Can you drive out around that time?"

"No problem," I replied.

She laughed. "Maybe you should pack a few things. We might be gone overnight." Suddenly she hesitated. "I mean if that is all right with you."

"Just great," I assured her.

She went on to explain that the next day being Sun-

day, there'd be no shooting. "And there is this lovely
mountain inn you simply must see. But with the drive
and all it would be too much to manage in one day.
You do understand, don't you?"

The fact that she was inviting me on an overnight
date did come as a delightful surprise, but I skipped
right past it. "See you at four, then," I said.

"Wonderful," she replied, and there was another
pause. "About last night. I'm sorry I had to be so
abrupt. You weren't angry?"

I laughed and she laughed back.

"See you at four," I repeated.

She whispered a soft goodbye, clicked off.

After lunch I stopped at the hotel's gift shop and
bought a small overnight bag, and at three I put another call through to the Marjoro Hotel in Dubrovnik.
No messages had come from Korla, and after remind-
ing the clerk where I could be reached, I tossed a
change of clothes and my shaving equipment into the
small bag. I wasn't worried in the event Korla called
and found me out. Cooling his heels a bit wouldn't
hurt, and frankly I was anxious to have some of Biro's
information on tap before getting down to the nitty-
gritty business of dealing with Korla.

I told the Fjord's clerk that I might be gone until the
following evening and to take any messages that may
come in. From here I went directly to the parking lot,
tossed my bag into the Fiat's luggage compartment and
took off. I made the ride out in less than a half-hour,
and when I pulled up alongside Biro's trailer it was a
few minutes after four. The trailer door opened and
Maya appeared, with Biro right behind. She wore a
pair of light beige slacks, sandals and a cream colored
blouse embroidered with sprays of flowers. Her long,
dark hair was caught up in a colorful silk handkerchief,
and she looked lovely.

I wondered what Biro might have thought of the
arrangements, and I found a chance to talk to him when

Maya stepped back inside the trailer to get her bag. I wanted him to know that the trip was Maya's idea, but that I was all for it myself.

"No sweat," he grinned. "She told me all about it." He put his hand on my shoulder, the way he had the day before. "She likes you, Nick. And so do I."

I used the opportunity to ask him if he had heard anything as yet from his partisan friends.

He shook his head. "But if I do, and if it's important enough, I know where to reach you. So relax and enjoy."

When Maya stepped out I took her bag and started for the Fiat. Suddenly Biro called out and dug into his pocket. He came up with the keys for his Mercedes and held them out. "Better take my jalopy," he said. "You'll be glad you did on those mountain roads."

He insisted, so I got my bag out of the Fiat, transferred it to the Mercedes, and put Maya's alongside. I then gave Biro the Fiat's keys, opened the passenger door to the Mercedes for Maya and then got in on the driver's side. I hit the ignition and the Mercedes purred to life. I released the handbrake and we were on our way.

We retraced the road to Kotor, following the highway north along the curving bay. Maya was in a real holiday mood, chatting easily and pointing things out along the way. We stopped briefly at Perast to fill the Mercedes' tank and then continued on to Risan, a pleasant seaside village. From here we turned off the main highway, our heading almost due west. Gradually, the narrow road became winding and steeper.

"Now the mountains," Maya bubbled. "Wait till you see them!"

She unknotted her scarf, shook her long hair loose and settled back against the seat, her head nestled lightly against my shoulder.

For the next half-hour the road spiraled upward. Now I knew why Biro had insisted that I take his car.

For the Fiat it would have been an uphill fight all the way, but the Mercedes easily maneuvered the steep, winding turns with the stealth of a jungle cat. At one point we passed a small mountain village with a road-sign that read: Alt. 1,290 meters—the equivalent of almost 4,000 feet.

Maya hugged my arm. "We're more than almost half-way there."

By now it was getting on to six. The sun had moved over to the left, pouring late afternoon shafts of golden light into the dark, wooded ravines below. Up ahead the road continued to wind and twist, uncoiling like a snake through the high mountain pass. So far the traffic had been exceptionally light, both ways, but as I banked into another curve I heard the muffled roar coming from behind. Instinctively, I touched the pedal and the Mercedes surged forward. I checked the rearview mirror, but the curve cut off the view from behind. I gave the pedal another tap.

Maya sensed something, touched my arm. "Is anything wrong?"

I shook my head vaguely. "Not sure ..." I rechecked the rearview mirror and a split second later the car came sweeping around the curve. I recognized it instantly—the same Porsche that had tailed me the day before. I gunned the pedal and the Mercedes lunged.

"Maya," I said firmly. "I want you to do something. Slide down in your seat, as far as you can. I want you to do it now!"

She hesitated.

"*Now*," I shouted. "NOW!"

She obeyed instantly.

"Good," I said reassuringly. "Just stay that way."

I had no idea where and how he had picked us up. It could have happened as far back as Perast when we stopped for gas. But that didn't matter now. What did matter was that I wasn't going to let him pull alongside for a clean shot. I thanked my lucky stars that Biro had insisted on my taking the Mercedes. At least we were decently matched.

My eyes flashed to the mirror. He was over to the left, but not quite all the way. I knew what he wanted—a fairly open stretch with enough passing room. That was his style, and he wouldn't make his move until the conditions were right. This guy was no compulsive gambler. He was a pro, instinctively cautious, and trained not to go beyond the calculated risk. Another curve loomed ahead. I banked into it and the Mercedes radials snarled with animal fury. But bad luck waited for me on the way out. Suddenly the road leveled and straightened out. It was exactly what the bastard needed. I groaned inwardly and tightened up on the wheel. I checked the rearview mirror. He was over the line, on my left, and coming up fast.

"Steady," I whispered to Maya. "Hold tight."

I came close to flooring the pedal and the Mercedes took off. Trees and rail posts flashed by. I kept checking the mirror. He was gaining slightly. I let him move up, timing it carefully. For a moment I lost him in the overhead mirror, but quickly picked him up in the sideview. He had shifted further to my left. So far so good. I backed off slightly on the gas, waited for him to close in. I rechecked the sideview mirror. When his front bumper drew up alongside my rear left fender, I cut the steering wheel right.

The Mercedes' tail swung left. It was a light enough bump, but the scream of metal filled the air as our fenders brushed momentarily. He didn't fall back, but came straight on. Again I cut the wheel right, hard. This time there was a solid, thudding crunch. His brakes howled when we broke loose and he was out of control. The crash when he hit the rail was deafening. I glimpsed him in the rearview mirror as he went over, a dark hurtling object falling away into the cavernous space below.

I brought the bucking Mercedes to a skidding halt along the narrow shoulder and leaped out.

"Stay inside," I cautioned Maya. "Stay put till I get back."

I pounded back down the road to where the Porshe had gone over. It lay upended on its front bumper on a slope about forty feet below, its rear precariously balanced against the trunk of a massive tree. Both doors had been blown open and a cloud of hissing, gray smoke issued from the shattered front end. I could see nothing of the driver.

There was a good chance he could have been thrown clear upon impact, but I couldn't be sure. And I had to be sure. I slipped Wilhelmina out of my shoulder holster, stepped over the railing and started down. Pebbles and loose soil fell away underfoot. I distinctly avoided a direct approach to the battered Porsche. Shifting to the left, I made a wide circling trek that would bring me to the rear of the vehicle.

The sun had almost set and the light was fading fast. Worse yet, a thin mist rising from the valley floor seeped upwards, blanketing the shadowy slope in a filmy haze.

I had hoped to find a corpse, but there was still no sign of him. I doubted very much that he was still in the car. In moments like this silence can become the fine edge between staying alive or getting oneself killed. I stepped into the shadows cast by a towering pine and waited. Actually, total silence doesn't exist, provided you listen with proper concentration. Gradually, from within the dark branches above, came the nervous flutter of birds. From the distant valley floor, came a farm dog's faint barks. Somewhere to my right, a small forest animal scurried unseen through a tangle of grass. At one point I heard my own breathing.

A car swept by on the highway above, tires hissing. Just as swiftly it faded off. Another sound emerged, a rustling, whisper light. It came from my left, somewhere off in the shadowed haze of brown earth and clumps of scattered shrubs. I turned my head toward the sound, not more than an inch, when the shot banged out. Bits of shattered bark spewed the air inches above my head.

I dropped to a crouch, darted to my right. I had barely glimpsed the spurt of orange-tongued flame, but I gauged the shot to have come from a patch of thick grass fringed by a mix of shale rock and powdery soil.

I circled the Porsche quickly and sped up a small slope that put me on slightly higher ground. A second later I spotted him. I was behind and above when he came inching out of the grassy patch. He was on his belly, dragging himself forward on his elbows. He must have sensed my position, because a second later his head snapped my way. I don't know how he managed it, but he hobbled to one knee, raising his bloodstained face in my direction. He brought the revolver up slowly, with great effort, and his hand shook violently. The advantage was definitely all mine, and I took it. I squeezed off two shots and he went over on his back, his arms flung outwards when he hit the ground.

I waited, slowly counting to ten. I approached from behind, dropping to one knee alongside his body. His eyes, bright with hate stared up into mine. A bloody froth oozed from the corners of his mouth. Suddenly his lower jaw twitched and his mouth snapped open; muscles strained, words struggled to tear loose. I leaned closer. He was trying to say something. It was garbled, totally without meaning. He coughed suddenly and blood welled from his gaping mouth. His eyes glazed over and his jaw fell slack.

I checked his pulse. It barely fluttered. I did what I'd do for any animal close to death and torn by pain. I touched the muzzle of my luger to his left temple and squeezed the trigger.

The shot echoed and reechoed for a long time. It still hummed in my ears as I trudged back up the slope to the highway. When I got there, I reholstered Wilhelmina and started back down the road toward the Mercedes. I could see the silhouette of Maya's head above the front seat. When I got back to the car and slipped in behind the wheel, she turned slightly. Most of her face was in shadow.

"Those shots?" she whispered.

I didn't even try to lie. "The man who tried to run us off the road is dead," I said simply. "It had to be done."

"Why?"

"For one thing he would have killed us. For another . . ."

I broke off and put my hands lightly on her shoulders. I kissed her on the forehead, and then lightly again on the lips. She didn't draw back. I knew her head must be full of questions, but there was nothing I could add by way of explanation at this point. It had turned out to be a bad scene, the very worst.

"Maybe we had better go back," I suggested.

She shook her head stubbornly, slipped her arms around my neck. "No," she said huskily. "Let's go on. Please . . ."

I started the Mercedes. We rolled gently off the shoulder and onto the road, driving for a while in silence. Along the horizon, above the shadowy bulk of a soaring mountain, an early star gleamed silver-bright in the darkening sky. It was quickly joined by another. I snapped on the headlamps and settled back against the seat. Hesitantly, she broke the silence.

"Only two questions. Do you mind?"

I shook my head and waited.

"Did you really come to Yugoslavia to buy furniture?"

I shook my head again.

"Is your name really Howard Kierzek?"

Another shake.

She smiled, slid close and put her head against my

shoulder as she had done earlier. "I trust you," she murmured. "And for now, no more questions. I promise."

About forty minutes later we turned into the inn's graveled driveway. A striking old building, it stood well off the road, its dark gabled roof silhouetted against a massive backdrop of moonlit clouds.

An elderly uniformed attendant met us when we pulled up to the door. I gave him the car keys and he said he'd have the luggage brought in. Maya took my hand eagerly and we went into the lobby, a spacious low-ceilinged room finished with smokey beams and furnished with oversized sofas and leather upholstered chairs. From a huge fireplace at the far end of the room, a crackling log fire threw leaping shadows across the paneled walls.

There was a bar off the lobby, and Maya suggested that I order something for myself and her while she checked the desk on the reservations she had made that morning. I was all for this. I was certainly in need of a drink.

The dimly lit bar was quiet when I entered. I ordered a scotch for myself, neat, and a fruit cordial for Maya. Before the drinks arrived, Maya returned. Everything at the desk was in order. Since we were both starved, I told the barman to have the drinks sent to our table and we left for the dining room. We ordered soup and a lamb and rice dish, and when the waiter left with our order the drinks arrived.

The meal did wonders for both of us. While we ate, sipping our drinks, Maya's cheerful nature showed signs of revival. All trace of what had happened back on the road seemed to have been forgotten. I was delighted. But the real surprise came at the end of the meal. When the waiter left the check and walked off, Maya leaned forward, placed a slender hand over mine.

"About our reservations," she said softly, and her

full lips curved into a slight, sly smile. "They had this one lovely, large room, so I thought—" Her hand pressured mine gently. "I thought you might like that, and I took it."

I tried hiding my surprise, tried poker-facing it, but something must have shown in my eyes. She started to withdraw her hand, but I caught it. It was just some of the things Biro had said about Maya, her trust she placed in people that made me wonder. The question came to my lips.

"Are you sure, Maya?"

Her smile deepened. She withdrew her hand, stood up. "Our room number is twenty-four. I'll need a little time."

I let a decent fifteen minutes go by before starting up. Room 24 was at the end of the long carpeted hallway on the second floor. The door was unlocked, and after entering I closed it gently behind me. Some light came from the partially opened bathroom door, enough to see by. From the bathroom came the sound of running water. I crossed the room to the large window and drew the drapes slightly. The spread had already been turned down on the large double bed, and our luggage was at the foot. I removed my jacket and found a hanger in the closet. I slung my shoulder holster over it, covered it with my jacket and hung it on the rack.

I removed my tie and shirt and suddenly the water was turned off. My pulse began to race. When the bathroom door swung open, I turned.

She stood in the doorway. The backlighting revealed all of her slender curves through the wispy, knee-length peignoir. She smiled, then seemed to float in my direction. Her arms encircled me. She pressed her cheek to mine and her delicate perfume flooded my senses.

"Disappointed?" she laughed.

I swept her up in my arms, carried her to the bed and eased her onto it.

I don't make love by the book. Doing it by the rules isn't my style. I kissed the smooth hollow of her throat, then moved to her mouth. She responded hesitantly at first, then more surely. Her arms tightened around my neck and her petal-smooth lips slowly parted. The tip of her warm tongue brushed mine, probed gently.

I let it build. There was time, endless time and I wanted both of us to savor every delicious moment. I undid the sash of the peignoir, swept the filmy garment aside. Her rose tipped breasts tilted temptingly toward me. I cradled the palm of my hand around one soft mound, felt a sensuous shiver race through her body. Lowering my head I grazed the fragrant, silky flesh with my lips. Gently, she slipped her hand over mine, guided the erect nipple to my mouth. I drew it in, felt her body arch. She moaned ecstatically.

The pace quickened. Her rhythmic body movements began, slowly at first—a subtle stirring from some mysterious inner source.

My hand moved across her curved hip, and I allowed my fingers to trace a path toward the inner regions of her satin smooth thighs. Gradually they parted, and I explored gently, intimately. My fingers became my eyes. Seeing what can't be seen. Feeling what can't be described. I probed deeper still and her movements quickened.

"Maya?"

"Yes," she whispered urgently. "*Yes.*"

I kicked off my shoes, unbuckled my belt and whipped off my pants.

When I moved over her again her body molded itself perfectly to mine. The rhythm began anew, increased. Tenderly she drew my head down, closed her lips over my mouth. A moment later her long, splendid thighs parted, made room.

Caught up, we moved together as one. We rose,

soared, fell back and soared again. She strained against me, moaning through clenched lips with every thrust I made. Gradually the abrupt movements changed, became a long sensuous glide. Our drift was earthbound, and we came to rest gently, lightly, with my head buried between her perfumed breasts.

For a long minute she lay perfectly still, then snuggled close. In the darkness, with my arms around her, I told her my name. It was all I could allow myself to tell her at this time, but we couldn't remain nameless strangers——not after what we had just shared.

"Nick," she murmured drowsily. "Nick . . . Carter." She brushed my shoulder with her lips, snuggled closer. "It's a lovely name. I like it very, very much . . ."

Her body went soft in my arms, and moments later she drifted off to sleep.

CHAPTER 11

The phone got us up a little after eight. It stood on a small table on Maya's side of the bed, and she stirred when I reached over her to answer its ring.

Biro's voice boomed in my ear. "Nick? That you?"

"Right."

He sounded excited.

"I hope it isn't too early, but things have been happening fast. I've just been in touch with some of my Yugoslavian friends and it looks like they've hit paydirt. They've located Korla's present whereabouts."

By now I was fully awake. "Where?"

"I'll give you the details when I see you. But there's something else. In fact, I was going to call you on this last night, but I figured, hell, it could hold till morning. Anyway, I had dinner at your hotel last night, and I thought I'd check with the desk to find out if you had any calls. The clerk said that a few had come in, all from the same guy. Only whoever it was, he wouldn't leave his name."

I was positive it had been Korla. It could mean that Salobin had finally arrived in the country, and it could also mean that Korla would be pressing hard now to close the deal. I knew I'd have to get cracking.

"Can I meet you back at the hotel?" I asked. "We'll leave here right after we've had some breakfast. I'll drop Maya off first at her place, and that should bring me back around one or so."

"I'll be there," he promised. He paused. "How's Maya?"

I grinned down at her and she smiled back.

"Lovely, but you know that."

He laughed, said something about driving carefully and clicked off. When I reached to replace the phone, she took my arm. A small frown creased her smooth brow. "Must we leave very soon?"

I kissed her lightly. "Not that soon."

The frown vanished and her full, lower lip trembled expectantly. When I placed my mouth over hers and nibbled gently, she pushed me off. I landed on my back and she quickly slid on top. She grinned down at me, giggling wickedly. Moments later her mouth closed over mine. A flame was kindled, became a roaring blaze. I made no effort to snuff it out . . .

Less than an hour later we were on our way, and Maya maintained a discreet silence about Biro's call as the Mercedes rolled up the miles. I was grateful for her tact. About an hour into the trip, when we approached the point where the shoot-out had taken place the night before, we were flagged down by a uniformed policeman. A road barrier had been set up alongside the point where the Porsche had gone over the guard rail, and a couple of other uniformed policemen, and a man in civilian clothes, were busy measuring the skid marks.

The policeman, a young man with startling blue eyes, asked to see my papers. I handed over my passport, and after he scanned through it he politely handed it back. Casually, I asked what the trouble was.

"A police matter," he smiled, and waved us on.

When we were on our way again, I glanced at Maya. She looked a bit pale and gave me a small, brave smile. Obviously she was as relieved as I was. The remainder of the trip went smoothly, and about an hour later we arrived in Kotor.

I dropped Maya off at her cottage, told her I'd be in touch and then drove directly to the hotel. I spotted my rented Fiat in the parking lot in the rear and pulled in alongside. It was a few minutes past one, and I headed straight for the bar. I recognized Biro's broad back hunched over a drink, and the moment he spotted me he was on his feet.

"Let's take a bottle and go to your room," he said after shaking hands. "There's a lot to tell."

Once in the room, Biro settled back in his chair, a tall drink clutched in his hairy fist.

"I didn't think my friends would nail it this soon," he chuckled, "but they've really put it together. Now for the nitty-gritty."

He got a map out from his pocket, unfolded it, and spread it out on the table between us. The map detailed the Yugoslavian-Adriatic coastline, and Biro stabbed a thick finger to the X he had pencilled between Dubrovnik and Cavtat. "You remember my telling you the other day that I was pretty sure that Korla maintained a coastal villa in the vicinity, don't you? Well, according to my informants I was right, and this is the precise location. From what they say, it's perched way up on one of those rocky cliffs with its back to the sea—it's fairly inaccessible."

He paused to take a long pull at his drink. "But that's only the tip of the iceberg. My friends also tell me that over the past few years, Korla's converted the place into a Goddamn fortress. It's loaded with electronic surveillance gear, and when Korla's in residence his armed guards patrol the turrets and the grounds around the clock. On top of that, right now, the number of guards seems to have been increased. So it could mean that they've got your Russian defector there after all."

He finished the drink and set the glass on the table. Gradually, his bushy brows puckered into a thoughtful frown. "I'm not getting nosey, Nick," he said slowly. "I know that this is your gig and you're going to have to tackle it the way you think best. But I can't help wondering. Are you seriously thinking of breaking into that place and somehow, someway, making off with the Russian?"

"You're a couple of light years ahead of me," I grinned. "Right now I only want to look the place over. Size it up. Just looking it over may offer some ideas. That's all I know right now. Time enough to decide later, right?"

He pumped his head thoughtfully, and when he reached for the bottle I thought it a good time to tell him about the shoot-out the day before, plus the one in the Beirut alley.

"It smells like the KGB," he said when I had finished. "There's a running war here between them and the UBDA, the secret Yugoslavian police. Actually, there's common talk around here that Moscow has placed some of their KGB agents inside the UBDA which gives them an inside track to a lot of things that are going on here. They've also got agents planted in factories and shops—moles who bury themselves in some obscure corner but who're ready to do their dirty work whenever they get the Kremlin call. The bartender downstairs could be one of them, or the waiter who served us dinner. You just can't be sure."

Sighing, he swung to his feet, putting a friendly hand on my shoulder. "If they're on to you, Nick, they're going to use every foul trick in the bag to get you out of the way and give them a clear field to get their runaway Russian back. It figures, and you know that as much as I do. Anyway, I want to go on helping. Anyway I can."

I walked him to the door, and he suddenly remembered something. Reaching inside his pocket, he came up with a snapshot of Korla's castle-styled villa taken by one of his Yugoslavian friends from a safe distance.

"You may find this useful," he explained, "along with the map."

I took it, thanked him, and then another thought seemed to cross his mind. "I almost forgot, but my friends also tell me that Korla's been going to Dubrovnik in the evenings. They think he's shacking up with a young actress, the wife of a local bureaucrat who spends a lot of his time in Zagreb. I don't know if it adds up to anything, but you never know what's useful in this business, right?"

I agreed, and after he gave my arm a friendly pat he left.

I locked the door behind him, and went back for another look at the map. A moment later the phone rang. It was Korla. He sounded annoyed and I let him rattle away.

"I've been trying to reach you since yesterday," he snarled. "First I called the hotel in Dubrovnik, and they gave me this number. So I called and they told me you were out. So I called again and kept calling and you were still out. And what are you doing in Kotor?"

"Visiting an old friend," I breezed back. "But why the beef? You said you weren't ready and that you'd get in touch when you were. Well, so where do we stand now?"

"Things are settled at this end," he said tersely. "We're ready to deliver. What about you? Has the money issue been cleared?"

"Not altogether," I lied. "After all, a contract this size can't be negotiated by my department head alone. Others have to be consulted. Besides, they're putting some pressure on me. They're asking that I be shown what I'm paying for before any money changes hands. Are you agreeable to that?"

"Not in the least," he snapped back.

"Then how can I be sure you really have our man?"

"You can't be," he replied. "That's the way it has to be. But once there is an agreement on price, and the money is on hand, ready to be delivered, you have my word that a suitable exchange procedure will be worked out to guarantee our mutual interests."

I came close to laughing into the mouthpiece. In my book, Korla's word was about as reliable as a three dollar watch. But since a payoff was something AXE would never consider, Korla's word was of no importance anyway. So I continued to stall.

"Look," I said in a friendly tone. "I'll get your message back to my people and we'll let them decide whether they want to go ahead on your terms. Let's see what they come up with. Frankly, I trust you all the way, and as soon as I know I'll—"

He cut me off. "Then you had better tell them this, too. Tell them I'm giving them precisely six days to come to a firm decision. At the end of that time I expect the money to be on hand. If it isn't, the deal is off and it will not be reopened. Do I make myself perfectly clear?"

"Perfectly," I echoed.

Moments after he hung up I reached for the bottle Biro had left behind and poured myself a drink. Admittedly, I was playing it close to the edge. So far, I only had Korla's word that he had Salobin, but on the evidence supplied by Biro's friends I was prepared to believe he was telling the truth. The fact that he had doubled his guard detail at the villa had to stand for something. Korla had to be protecting something a hell of a lot more important than his wine cellar to take such precautions.

Later that afternoon I called Maya, and though I really ached to see her I had to turn down her invitation for dinner at her place. With Korla calling the shots, and only six days to get something going, I needed the time to rough out some preliminary plan. But there was one thing I was sure of, and when I told Maya that I'd be leaving the following morning, it took her by surprise.

"But it won't be for too long," I added quickly. "Two, three days at the most."

"Good," she whispered. "And you will call when you get back? Right away?"

"Absolutely."

She paused slightly. "You will be careful . . . please . . ."

I assured her I would. I waited until I heard her click off before hanging up.

I left Kotor a little past noon on the following day, the luggage section of the Fiat crammed with camping gear I had bought earlier that morning at a local sporting goods shop. Besides a portable butane stove and a supply of fuel cartridges, I had bought a short-handled axe, an army-type mess kit, a three-celled flashlight, a fiber-filled sleeping bag and a lightweight, aluminum-framed backpack.

I had also bought a pair of hiking boots, a pair of cavalry twill pants and a chamois shirt. I changed into these in a room in the rear of the shop, and then made two final purchases—a pair of thermos bottles that came packed in their own kit, and Zeiss 10-powered, 25mm wide-angled binoculars. After I paid, I stopped at another shop—a combination grocery and deli—and picked up an assortment of canned food and a couple of jars of instant coffee. The shopkeeper, an elderly man with bushy brows, obligingly filled both thermos bottles with clear, sparkling water.

I took the same road out of town I had used coming in, recrossing the railroad tracks where the policeman had given me directions only a few days before. Once I was on the highway, I followed the curving bay. At intervals, I kept a check on the rearview mirror. Nothing suspicious turned up, so I took my time. When I got to Cavtat, it wasn't quite two. I drove down the town's principle cobblestoned street and pulled up before a small restaurant. I had a quick lunch of thick bean soup served with half a loaf of dark, crusty bread. It wasn't quite 2:30 when I was back on the road, my heading due north. I really didn't have too much further to go. I drove through Cilipi, an even smaller village than Cavtat.

From here the road began to dip, threading its way along a valley floor flanked by wooded hills. For a while I lost all view of the Adriatic. Terraced vineyards dotted some of the slopes, but there were few signs of habitation. About twenty minutes later, as I came out of the turn, the sea suddenly reappeared on my left. A moment later I spotted the soaring cliff with Korla's turreted castle crowning the summit. Its massive stone towers were silhouetted starkly against the brilliant blue sky.

I pulled over to the side of the road, braked, and got out the snapshot Biro had given me. It was one and the same, no doubt about it. I got the binoculars out of the glove compartment and gave the place a few searching sweeps. The outer wall that enclosed the sprawling building was at least forty feet high. Turrets were spaced out at about twenty-foot intervals, and I zeroed in on one of them with my binoculars. A bearded man's head and shoulders showed above the crenelated stonework. If he were armed, I couldn't see it, but I assumed he was. I carefully checked the other turrets. Each one of them posted a lookout. I figured the turrets atop the adjacent walls were similarly posted with guards. For the moment, I had seen enough.

After I slipped the binoculars back inside the glove compartment, I started up the Fiat. I kept the speed under 25 mph, scarcely giving the castle a second glance as I drew abreast and slid by. I was looking for something else, and about a half-mile up the road I got lucky. It was a large, open field, lumpy and weed-covered, but at the far end, it bordered a patch of heavy woods. It was made to order. I checked the road both ways. No traffic was in sight, coming or going. I cut the Fiat's wheels hard right, fed gas. I came off the road fast, bouncing over the low shoulder and onto the field.

The spunky little car lurched and swayed, its springs groaning like an animal in pain. As I drew close to the edge of the field I spotted a break between the trees and headed for it. I gauged the opening to be wide enough to take the Fiat and inched forward. Overhanging branches from the nearest trees scraped noisily across the roof as I edged in. I kept easing forward until the Fiat was fully under. When the branches stopped scraping, and had sprung back to their original position, I cut the ignition, braked and got out.

I walked to the field for a quick look. The low-hanging branches screened practically all the Fiat, and all I could see through dense foliage were a few glints of reflected sunlight off the bumper chrome. From the road, it would be absolutely undetectable.

So far, so good. Now I was ready for stage two. I got the fully-loaded backpack out of the luggage and buckled up. Hopefully, I'd look like a tourist on a countryside hike. I crossed the field, and when I reached the road I turned left, heading back in the direction from which I had come. About fifteen minutes later I was about back to the castle. It was well off to my right, the sunlight tossing bright reflections off the windows. I walked right past it as though it didn't exist.

About five minutes later I crossed to the left side of the highway and entered the woods that flanked the shoulder. I found a narrow foot trail and plodded along as it led to higher ground. It was fairly steep going, but my cleated hiking boots were a big help. I was puffing slightly when I came out above the tree line, and I stopped for a look around. I had judged things rather well. From where I stood I had a fairly unobstructed view of the castle, but with enough distance in between to prevent my being seen.

Satisfied, I continued the climb for about another fifty feet. To my left was an outcropping of massive boulders. Unbuckling my pack, I squatted down, got out the binoculars, and focused on the castle.

Intelligence gathering can be a pretty dull business, and I had a feeling I was in for a long, tedious session. I kept scanning the castle at regular intervals, but there were absolutely no signs of any activity. An hour crawled by. Nothing. Another forty-five minutes. Still nothing. I lit my third or fourth cigarette and took a few turns around the area to work the cramped feeling out of my legs. I was feeling a little hungry, and was thinking of getting something out of the pack, when a small burst of sunlight flared up along the castle's front wall.

I snapped the binoculars to my eyes, zeroed in. A second burst of light followed. It came from a pair of glass French doors that had suddenly been opened. The doors led out to a small stone balcony, and a man stepped into view. There was no mistaking him. It was Korla. His bloated features floated before my eyes, seemingly close enough for me to be able to reach out and pluck the thick cigar that drooped between his lips.

He stood there for a minute or so, then ground out the cigar on the balcony's ledge and tossed it over the side. Turning, he reentered the room. Another spurt of reflected sunlight flared as the glass doors closed behind him. The long wait had paid off. Korla's presence had been confirmed and I was more convinced than ever that Salobin was somewhere on the premises. But just where posed a lot of problems. I figured the castle to have as many as eighty rooms, maybe more, and locating in just which room Salobin might be kept prisoner would take a lot of doing. But before I could even begin searching the rooms, I'd have to get inside the castle. How? At that moment, I didn't even have the germ of an idea.

For one thing, there were the security guards. According to what Biro's friends had reported, the place was crawling with them. So even if I did manage to get inside the place and begin a room-by-room search for Salobin, how far would I get before Korla's men would be on to me? At the most I'd have ten minutes. But even if I got lucky and did locate Salobin, where would it get me? If getting in would be tough, getting out would be tougher yet. With the place loaded with electronic surveillance devices, we'd end up as fat targets for Korla's gun-toting goons.

"Nick," I said to myself, "there just has to be a better way." I sighed inwardly. "Okay, what?" I shook my head. I had no idea.

I drove the questions out of my mind and swung to my feet. I trudged around to get the circulation back in my legs, and then I remembered I hadn't eaten. I got a can of dried beef from the pack and a package of biscuits. What I really needed was a cup of black coffee, but I had left the portable stove in the Fiat, and I didn't want to risk an open fire. I ate slowly, my back up against one of the boulders and the binoculars hanging by their neck cord across my chest. When I was finished, I kicked some dirt loose with the heel of my boot, deep enough to bury the empty can. I took a few swallows of water from my thermos and lit up a cigarette. The long wait went on.

At a little past six the sun was well over to my left. The slanted rays backlighted the castle and the encircling wall took on a purplish hue. It wouldn't be long before dusk would set in, and I was ready to call it quits for the day and head back for the car. I was about to buckle on the backpack when two pinpoints of light showed up behind the castle's main gate. I dropped the pack, grabbing the binoculars. It was a car, a big black limo, and though the light was dimming it had the same familiar lines of the one Korla had used in Beirut. Moments later the gates swung open and the car rolled through. When it cleared the gates it stopped, and the driver got out.

I recognized him instantly. It was the big guy, the chauffeur who came close to strangling me after I had slapped Korla the night we had met at the inn. He came around to the front of the car and squatted down to check the left tire. A moment later the rear window rolled down and Korla's head popped into view. He seemed to shout something at the chauffeur, and the big guy straightened up in a hurry, ran around to the driver's side and hopped back in.

I watched them through the glasses as the car slowly made its way down the winding, graveled driveway. When it reached the highway it turned left and headed north toward Dubrovnik.

I put the glasses down and settled back against the boulder. It was just 6:30, and it squared away with the report Biro had received from his Yugoslavian friends that Korla would take off each evening around this time for a presumed roll in the hay with the bureaucrat's straying wife. If it were true, it would be another piece of information worth considering, but just where it might fit in, I couldn't imagine. Meanwhile, I changed plans about heading back for the Fiat. I had to know when Korla would return.

It turned out to be another long wait. The night turned particularly dark, with no moon and only a sprinkling of stars. I could just barely make out the distant cliff, and almost nothing of the castle, except for a few lights at some scattered windows.

At intervals I dozed off, but just for brief moments. Time dragged. By ten o'clock the traffic on the highway was almost nonexistant. Occasionally a car would flash by, its headlights piercing the thin mist that seeped down from the wooded slopes.

Midnight came and went. I began to wonder if Korla would be gone all night. A half-hour later, when I was beginning to get very restless, I heard the car. Seconds later the headlights stabbed the velvety darkness. I raised the binoculars to my eyes. I watched the limo as it slowed down, following it as it made its turn off the highway and onto the graveled driveway that wound its way to the castle. I continued to watch as it made its climb up the gravel path. The castle's gates, undoubtedly electronically controlled, swung open as the car approached. It passed through, its taillights glowing like twin coals. Slowly, the gates swung shut.

I checked the luminous hands of my watch. It was almost one. Korla had been gone about six hours. Either the girl was very good, or Korla needed a lot of recovery time. Frankly, I was too tired to give the subject much thought as I carefully made my way down the slope. When I reached the tree line I got out the flashlight to help me locate the foot trail. I found it soon enough and quickly made it back to the road. About fifteen minutes later I reached the field where I had parked the Fiat.

I was too tired to bother making coffee. I got the sleeping bag out of the luggage, spread it out on the ground, unzipped it and slipped in.

A forest is never totally silent. I heard running water, probably a brook somewhere. A tree toad peeped sharply and his lady love peeped back. Maya came to mind. I vividly recalled our night together at the inn and the way her delicately scented body had molded itself to mine. Her sexuality had taken me by surprise, but in a most pleasant way. Her face floated before my closed eyes as I drifted off into sleep.

CHAPTER 12

I awoke with the birds and located the stream I had heard during the night. I splashed some water on my face, brushed my teeth and refilled both thermos bottles. When I returned, I got out the small butane stove, primed it, and soon had a fire going. Breakfast was instant coffee, a tin of smoked sardines and another package of crackers. I made a careful job of cleaning up, then replaced the stove in the car's luggage section and buckled on my pack. I made up a whole thermos of black coffee to take along. It wasn't much after seven when I started out. I crossed the field, retracing the steps I had taken the day before. The castle showed no activity when I walked briskly by, and soon afterward I found the narrow foot trail that led to the woods.

I took my position as before, my back against one of the boulders and the binoculars slung across my chest. At intervals I scanned the castle's walls and windows but didn't catch a glimpse of any sign of life until around noon, when a tall, bearded guy came out through the gate leading a large Doberman. The dog pranced, high-stepping from the end of its leash, and the man kept tugging at it to keep the skittish animal in line. The pair quickly rounded the castle's outer wall and that was the last I saw of them.

During the next two hours nothing happened. But, at 2:30, a small delivery van turned off the highway and slowly made its way up the castle's graveled driveway. I checked it through the binoculars. Lettered on the side of the van in the Cyrillic alphabet were the words: *Govedina & Svinjetina*—"beef and pork." Obviously Korla was laying in some provisions.

When the gates swung open, the van quickly passed through and the gates closed. About twenty minutes later the van reappeared at the gates and was let out. It took its time coming down the fairly steep drive, then turned right at the highway and headed south. I checked my watch. It was just 3:00. I had finished off most of the coffee by now and was feeling hungry. I rummaged through the pack and selected a tin of canned beef, opening it with one of those little metal keys and spooned some out. It was over salted and greasy. I ate less than half and buried the rest. It took two cigarettes to kill the taste.

By six, my leg muscles were cramped with fatigue. Dusk was coming on fast and the sky first turned fawn color behind the castle's soaring turrets, then a blushing pink as the sun started to set. I was a bit curious by now. Would the previous evening's scenario be repeated? I didn't have long to wait. About twenty minutes later the glow of distant headlamps approached the castle's gates.

When the gates swung open, Korla's limo moved out and down the winding driveway. At the highway it promptly turned left.

It gave me something to think about. Once doesn't mean always, but twice in a row suggests a pattern. It was imput data that could be useful. Meanwhile, I had another long wait ahead of me.

It was close to 1:00 again, and I was down to the last cigarette in my pack when the limo finally returned I watched it snake its way back up the driveway and through the open gates into the darkness beyond. I was ready to close shop for the night. I stood up, buckled on my backpack and then carefully groped my way back down the slope. I soon made it back to the Fiat. I was really bushed by the time I got out the sleeping bag and must have dropped off to sleep only seconds after I crawled in and zipped up.

I awoke early again the following morning, but was in no hurry about getting back to my spotter's position on the slopes. I got the stove going, heated up some water and shaved by means of the Fiat's sideview mirror. All at once I hungered for a decent meal, so I tossed my gear into the Fiat's luggage section and took off. After crossing the lumpy field I turned right and headed for Dubrovnik.

I made it in around forty minutes and found a parking spot in front of a restaurant on Prijeko, one of Dubrovnik's main thoroughfares. My outdoor table offered a good view of the Sponza Palace with its huge clock tower. After I had finished off a platter of scrambled eggs and spicy sausage, plus two cups of really great coffee, I was feeling a lot better. I also figured it was a good time to try and contact Biro. There was a phone kiosk to one side of the dining area, but when I failed to reach Biro at his hotel, I had the operator route the call to his mobile camper on location. At the third ring he picked it up, recognizing my voice instantly.

"Christ, buddy!" he boomed. "You've had us worried!"

I told him where I was, but since it was a public phone I went very easy on the details. I told him I had a few more things to check out at this end before starting back for Kotor.

"Have you come up with anything definite so far?" he asked.

"Maybe," I replied. "Just maybe."

I then switched subjects and asked about Maya.

"She's fine," he assured me, "but a little anxious about seeing you. Can I tell her when?"

"Right now, I'd say tomorrow evening sometime. Around eight."

We hung up shortly afterward, and I spent most of the late morning and afternoon on a walking tour of the city. Around five I got back to the Fiat, stopped briefly at a gas station to fill up, and then headed south again for Korla's castle. Traffic remained light, and though I kept a constant eye out for a possible tail, I saw nothing.

It wasn't quite an hour later when I carefully eased the Fiat into its old hiding place under the trees at the far end of the field. I cut the ignition and checked my watch. It wasn't quite six, but the shadows were lengthening and a few stars already showed in the mauve sky. I didn't bother with the backpack, but I took the binoculars.

I crossed the field, then followed it along the edge where it bordered the highway's shoulder. I kept within the shadow of the tangled weeds when I passed the castle, kept going straight until I reached the familiar break in the trees where the foot trail led upwards. This time, however, I didn't take it all the way up. About half-way up, I found a point that gave a fair view of the castle's gravel driveway.

I checked my watch. It was 6:25. Less than five minutes later I felt my pulse starting to race as the two tiny beams of light appeared behind the castle's shadowy gates. I raised the binoculars to my eyes, watching the black limo make its slow descent. Once again it turned north toward Dubrovnik.

I let the binoculars go slack on its cord and dug into my pocket for a cigarette. I lit up, took a deep drag and let the smoke come out slowly. When something happens three nights running you've got to believe that more than just chance is involved. I had spotted a pattern. Actually, it didn't matter whether Korla was really screwing the bureaucrat's wife, or sitting up with a sick friend. But what did matter was that each night, for three nights running, he had left his fortress at a precise time and returned at an equally predictable time. It was a starting point of a kind, something to build on.

When Biro had asked me whether I had come up with anything definite, I had still drawn nothing but blanks. But now something had started to sprout. Admittedly, it was a wild idea, but I was scarcely in a position to be choosy. As I worked my way back down the slope, heading back for the Fiat, I began giving my plan serious thought.

I got back and was inside the sleeping bag, but tonight I didn't fall asleep easily. For more than an hour I kept toying with ideas, checking the possibilities against the percentages of pulling it off. No matter how I figured it, the odds remained staggering. "Nick," I said to myself, "you've got to be crazy. You've gone strictly bananas on this one."

Bananas or not, I couldn't shake it loose.

The following morning I was off to an early start. I didn't bother with any breakfast. I threw the sleeping bag into the luggage compartment and backed the Fiat out from under the trees. I got back on the highway, heading south. I passed the castle, still shrouded in morning mist and sped right by. I watched the sun come up, the broad shafts of light turning the Adriatic into burnished gold. I drove through a small number of villages, until I came to Cavtat, the town where I had stopped for lunch when I had first set out for Korla's castle.

Cavtat is a combination fishing village and resort, and I remembered seeing a number of marinas when I had driven through the first time. Turning off the main cobblestoned street, I drove to the docks that lined the picturesque bay. Boats of every description, powered as well as sails, bobbed and swung on their anchor chains. I parked in an open area alongside a stack of lobster traps and got out.

A row of weathered jetties extended into the sea, each with its own docking site. The second one looked interesting. There was a shack at the far end, and when I was about half-way there, an old man appeared in the doorway.

He was rake thin, and when he shuffled up, he doffed his cap politiely. *"Dobro jutro,"* he greeted me. He seemed very anxious to please.

I glanced at some of the boats tied up at the far end of the jetty. *"Camci u zakup,"* I asked. "Were any of the boats for hire?"

I had already spotted something that interested me—a compact flybridge-cabin boat that was moored at the far end of the jetty. I pointed to it and asked if that one was available.

"Da," he grinned. It was, and he went on to say that it had just been brought in that morning by an Englishman who had rented it for two weeks. When we walked down the jetty to get a closer look, I liked it even more. By the way it sat on the water, I could tell that it had a shallow draught, which made it even more suitable for the purpose I had in mind.

The rental rate by the day was 300 dinars—about twenty-five dollars. I told him I was interested, and that I'd take it for the day on a trial basis. If I liked it, I might go with it for the rest of the week.

He pumped his head eagerly and his friendly grin widened. He said he'd have it fueled up and ready to go in less than an hour. I thanked him and told him I'd be back after I had something to eat.

I had breakfast in a nearby dockside restaurant, and by the time I'd eaten and paid the check, more than half an hour had gone by. I did a few turns around the dock area and then strolled back to the marina. When I walked out on the jetty the old man waved in greeting. Everything was ready to go. I got out my wallet and peeled off three 100-dinar notes to cover the day's rental. He thanked me, pocketed the bills and handed over the keys.

"*Srécan put*," he smiled. "Have a nice trip." I thanked him and hopped aboard.

The engines responded nicely when I hit the ignition, and I headed north, in the direction of Korla's castle. I was in no great rush, and I intended to take some time to test the boat's responses. It didn't take much to know that I had a good boat under me.

I heeled sharply from starboard to port a couple of times to check the degree of list it would take, and she righted herself remarkably well and fast each time. Power was no problem either. I put her through a few deep S-curves, and the twin diesels delivered with an authoritative growl at the slightest touch of the throttle.

Once I had put her through her paces, I settled for a cruising speed, and about an hour-and-a-half later, I approached the castle atop the cliff high above the sea. I cut back on the speed, and as I slid past, I focused in on it with my binoculars. The back view was no more revealing than the front. From the castle's base, the rocky cliff dropped almost perpendicularly into the sea. There was no beach, just a surrounding jumble of partially submerged boulders awash in the foaming surf.

About a mile beyond the castle, I spun the wheel hard, completing a full U-turn. On the way back, after I had passed the castle, I began to edge in toward shore. This particular stretch of coastline is dotted with coves and inlets, and I explored several before finding one to my liking. It was located about three miles below the castle, which made it close enough, and it was fairly free of rocks. What I liked in particular was that it was deep enough to bring the boat right in to shore without the risk of grounding it.

As I nudged up against the embankment, I cut the engines and listened. From beyond the weed covered shore came the distant hum of traffic, the occasional whine of tires. I judged the highway to be less than fifty yards away. It was perfect.

One of the final things I did before leaving was to locate the inlet's position on one of the sea maps I found in the desk drawer of the boat's cabin. When I had the information right, I jotted down the longitude and latitude. As seas go, the Adriatic isn't very wide, and at this point, the Italian coastline was no more than 120 nautical miles due west at the very most. After I made a note of this in my pad, I started up the engines, slipped the boat through a tight U-turn and headed out to sea again.

The wind was to my back, and with the boost from a fast moving current, I was able to make the return trip to Cavtat in just a bit over an hour. When I *put-putted* up to the jetty, the old man was already out of the shack. He waved, and a moment later he caught the line I threw him and secured me snugly alongside.

I liked everything about the boat, and when I followed him into the shack I told him that I'd take it for the next five days. I also told him that it might take a day or two before I'd be getting back, but that he was to refill the tanks, plus the spares, and have everything ready to go no matter when I'd show up. To ease his mind, I told him I was prepared to pay him in advance. He grinned happily, pumping his head up and down and said *"Da, Da"* repeatedly. Everything, he assured me, would be just the way I wanted it.

Satisfied, I got out my wallet and handed over three 500-dinar notes to cover the rental. I also peeled off an extra fifty and held it out to him, but he politely shook his head and refused. I tried imagining a New York cabbie or head waiter refusing a tip. Impossible!

I killed the next few hours hanging around town. I was very eager to get back to Maya, but a nagging uncertainty had to be resolved. I wandered around the town's narrow, winding streets, peering into shop windows, and finally stopped for a bite at a small restaurant. I ordered a lamb dish with rice and a bottle of local beer. I ate slowly and it was around five when I got up to pay the check. It came to a bit over a dollar, including the state service charge. Incredible.

When I got back to the Fiat and started up, the tank registered less than a quarter full. I found a service station just outside town, filled up, and then headed north, back in the direction of Korla's castle. It was a few minutes past six when I zipped past the place, but this time I didn't see the need of concealing the Fiat between the trees on the far side of the deserted field. Instead, I continued on for about a quarter of a mile, and then pulled over to the side and parked beneath the shadow of a massive, roadside oak.

I killed the engine and waited. At intervals I glanced into the sideview mirror that gave an unobstructed view of the road behind. Traffic was light as usual. Gradually, the dusk closed in, mantling the distant hills and peaks in a misty, purplish haze. Soon I heard the thin whine of approaching tires. I checked the mirror just in time to see the headbeams arcing the dark as the car cut onto the highway. I slumped down in the seat. Moments later Korla's familiar limo swept by. I let out a sigh of relief as I watched it speed off to Dubrovnik.

I waited until the taillights vanished before starting up the car. Cutting hard, I made a U-turn and headed south.

I was glad I had double-checked. This was the fourth night running that Korla had taken off. The pattern was holding. It was as much as I could hope for. I toed the accelerator and the Fiat responded smartly. I rolled down the driver's window and listened to the wind rushing by. All at once I was in one hell of a hurry to get back to Maya.

It was almost 8:30 when I arrived in Kotor, and I drove directly to Maya's small cottage. The place looked dark when I pulled around to the side of the house, but when I braked and switched off the ignition, the small, overhead porch light glowed on. I got out, slamming the door shut behind me and went around to the front. Before I could ring, the door opened slightly.

"Nick?" came the low whisper.

I stepped into the darkness, kicking the door shut. A moment later her naked body was in my arms, her head buried against my chest.

"I was worried," she whispered. "Biro told me you would be returning tonight. I was hoping you would come here first and . . ."

We kissed lightly and I drew her close, her soft, rounded breasts straining against me. Her tongue glided into my mouth. Drawing back, she quickly slipped her hand in mine.

"Come," she pleaded.

She led the way through the narrow dark hallway and into the dimly lit bedroom. Her hair hung loose and free. She smiled, then offered her mouth. We kissed repeatedly. When we finally broke and she moved toward the bed, I probably executed the fastest strip I had ever done in my life. When I joined her on the bed she hovered above me.

"Let me," she whispered. "Please . . ."

She began with feathery kisses. First my mouth, then on to my throat and chest, her scented breasts moving lightly across me. Fiery currents rippled through me, fanning out in all directions. By the time her moist lips touched my groin, I was as ready as I'd ever be.

She gave a little cry, buried her head lower yet. The

fiery currents became rivers of flame. I caught her up, rolled her under me. Our mouths locked. Gently, her slender legs slid upwards along my thighs and she opened to me. She was all giving, all churning motion. We moved as one as wave after wave of sensual pleasure pounded through our bodies. At the very end she moaned deeply, gave a final convulsive shudder and relaxed in my arms.

I pushed a damp lock of hair from her forehead and kissed her lightly on the lips.

She smiled. "Are you going to run off again? Right away?"

I shook my head, pressed my lips against her open mouth.

CHAPTER 13

I was awakened a little after seven by Maya's soft kiss on my cheek. She was up and dressed, smiling radiantly as she held out my shaving kit.

"I knew you'd be wanting this, so I brought it from the car. And now, what would you like for breakfast?"

I thanked her, and told her that coffee and toast would be enough. I was rather eager to see Biro on some final points.

While Maya left for the kitchen, I went to the bathroom. I lathered up, shaved quickly and somehow managed to nick myself not only once, but twice. I splashed cold water on my face, toweled myself dry and went out to the kitchen. Coffee was on the table, and a pan of scrambled eggs was on the stove.

Maya kissed me on the mouth. "Toast is not enough for a man to start his day," she laughed. "Start pouring your coffee and I'll get some plates."

The eggs were excellent, as was the coffee. We sat opposite each other in the small sunlit kitchen, and though I tried to hide it, she must have sensed my restless thoughts. Our time together was swiftly running out, and there was little—nothing, in fact—that I could do to extend it.

Suddenly, she covered my hand with hers. "What is it, Nick? I don't want you to tell me what you can't. But I am worried. About you. About so much . . ."

There was very little I could say. "I know you're imagining all sorts of things," I said quietly, "terrible things, perhaps." I paused, searching for the right words, and her clear violet eyes never left mine. "I'm in Yugoslavia on a very delicate matter," I continued. "All I can say is that an elderly man is being held a prisoner here, and friends of his in my country have asked me to help if I can. It requires sensitive negotiations, and as you know from the experience we had when we were driving to the inn, there are others who would do everything to keep me from succeeding."

She nodded thoughtfully, then frowned. "But then why not go to the police? Surely, this would be a matter for them."

I shrugged. "Ordinarily, yes. But not in a matter of this kind. There are areas in which the police can't help. In fact, all involvement must be avoided. And this is one of them. Trust me on that."

She sighed, squeezed my hand. "I trust you. But if there were some way I could help—no matter what it was—all you have to do is ask."

I got up and went around to her side of the table. She stood up and for several moments I held her close. "Thank you, Maya," I whispered.

She grinned up at me. "And now you must go again. Isn't that so?" She was forcing herself to be cheerful, and I loved her all the more for it.

While Maya cleared the table, I went into the bedroom and phoned Biro's hotel, but the clerk said he had already left for work. I thanked him and hung up. I offered to drive Maya out to location, but there were some things she had to do and she didn't want to hold me up. We walked out to where I had parked.

"Come back tonight," she said. "Please . . ."

I promised I'd try. It was the best I could do.

Less than twenty minutes later I had parked the Fiat behind Biro's mobile camper. I knocked on the door and Biro opened up, a steaming cup of coffee clutched in his hairy fist.

"*Christ!*" he bellowed. "Long time no see."

Closing the door behind us, he waved to a chair piled with magazines and newspapers. Scooping them up, he tossed them on the littered table, then went to the bubbling coffee maker and began pouring another mug.

"Okay," he said handing it to me, "is there anything you'd like to talk about? Not that you have to."

I grinned, then took a sip of the scalding coffee. Despite his gruff approach, Biro fully respected my right to say nothing. Accordingly, I told him what I felt to be best at the moment; his Yugoslavian friends had provided productive information—up to a point.

"And the Russian," Biro asked. "Do you think Korla has him in the castle?"

I nodded. "Positive. I can't see it any other way. Anyway, it's what I'm counting on."

"So you've come up with something? Some practical plan?"

"Hardly practical," I admitted. "What I'm going on is part conjecture, part intuition and part calculated guess. But it's all I've got. Naturally I'd like having more, but you know the game. When time's running out, you go with what you've got."

He scowled over his mug. "I know exactly what you mean, Nick. Hawk and I faced plenty of situations like this back in the war." He paused, and his bushy brows knotted thoughtfully. "But what about the other business, Nick? I mean those three attempts to wipe you out. It's part of the imput data you've got to consider."

I hadn't forgotten. Still, for reasons I couldn't figure out, they hadn't come after me since the night on the road with Maya. Of course, that in no way meant they had called it quits, and I wouldn't allow myself to believe that for a minute. But they were holding off, and I was damned happy about it. For one thing, it had given me the necessary time to concentrate fully on Korla. Meanwhile, there was something I needed from Biro, and I went right into it.

"I'm going to need some extra fire power," I said, "and I'm going to need it fast. In fact, I doubt if I have the time to make a request through the usual channels. But with your shooting a war movie, and from what I've seen, I was wondering—"

"Hell, yes," he chuckled. "You've come to the right guy. Our property department's loaded. It's a regular arsenel. A lot of it is blank ammo, of course, but we've got the live stuff for when we go for extreme realism in some of the scenes. Naturally, it's mostly World War II hardware, but you're welcome to whatever you want."

When I told him that that would be fine, he grabbed the phone and was soon through to his property man. "Ryan," he barked, "I'm sending someone right over. Give him anything he wants. I mean *anything*. Rifles, ammo, grenades, whatever. You got that?"

Biro paused to listen, grunted a few times, then hung up.

"It's all set," he grinned. "Take anything you want, and don't worry about Ryan. He was a sergeant who served with our outfit back in the OSS days, and he knows what a buttoned-up lip means. He probably won't even tell me what you took."

When we left the camper, Biro pointed out the

property shed, a Quonset hut at the far end of the open field.

"Come by when you're through," he said, "and we'll have some lunch in the commissary."

I thanked him and hopped into the Fiat. When I started up the engine, he pushed his craggy face through the open driver's window. "It's Maya," he said seriously. "I think she's gone bananas over you, Nick. How much does she really know? About *you?*"

"Only my name. I hate doing it that way, but the mask stays on. It has to, right?"

"No other way," he replied. "And it's got to be tough on you, too." He shook his head, sighed and stepped back. I toed the gas pedal and he waved as I took off.

When I braked in front of the property building, Ryan, a peppery-looking little guy in his early fifties, was waiting for me at the door. We shook hands briefly, and he led the way inside. As Biro had said, the place was a regular arsenel. The choice in rifles alone was staggering. The narrow aisles were lined with racks stacked with Gerands, Enfields, Mausers, plus some Carcanos and Mannlichers. The same was true of the machineguns—row after row of Stens, Schmiesers and American Thompsons.

I slipped a Thompson off its rack, checked the sights. The Thompson has a fairly short barrel, is on the light side, and though its accuracy at middle and far range isn't the greatest, its fire power on full automatic is devestating.

"How about live ammo for this?" I asked.

"As much as you want," Ryan replied. "You say how much, you got it."

I told Ryan I'd take the Thompson, and that I'd like a half-dozen oversized clips of ammo. He nodded, and the shopping tour continued.

There were some Very signal type pistols on a shelf,

so I took one, plus a box of flare cartridges to match. I also selected a small battery-operated bullhorn and a fifty-foot coil of thin but tough nylon rope. There was only one item left.

"Would you happen to have any smoke grenades?" I asked.

Ryan grinned. "How many do you want? Fifty? A hundred? We're loaded to the gills."

I laughed, told him a few would be fine, and he came up with four. We then made a package of the works, wrapping all of it up in a couple of large, green plastic sheets that I carred out and stuffed into the Fiat's cramped luggage compartment.

Ryan waved as I drove off. Biro's description of the wiry Irishman was more than apt. He never once inquired why I wanted the stuff, or who I was. Unfortunately, competent people like Ryan are in short supply these days.

At the last minute I decided against having lunch with Biro. Time was running short. I did stop by his camper, though, to thank him for his help, past and present.

"Then how about dinner tonight?" he asked.

I shook my head. "I can't. In fact, I may have to drop out of sight again for a couple of days."

"So this time it's down the pipe all the way." He stuck out his hand. "Whatever you're getting into, Nick, the best of luck."

We shook on it.

I was soon on my way back to the hotel. When I arrived, I got the bundle out of the Fiat's trunk, went directly to my room and locked the door behind me.

AXE's cryptology division is first rate. Ordinarily, I prefer direct communication with either Hawk or a local AXE agent no matter what part of the world I may happen to be in. But there are times when this just isn't practical. This was one of them. To speak to Hawk directly would mean getting to a scrambler phone to insure total privacy, and the nearest one would be in the U.S. Consulate in Belgrade and I didn't have time to make the trip. In our last telephone conversation, Korla had given me six days to come up with the money and we were already into the fifth day. The only other choice I had was to go with the code book.

Basically, AXE's code makes use of the three-in-one system, a combination of numerals, symbols and various phrase and phonic combinations. To make it additionally fail-safe, the system is juggled about every six months.

For the next three hours I labored over my memo pad, covering sheet after sheet of paper until I had boiled the message down to about a half-page. I then burnt all of the notes I had made, put the final message inside my jacket pocket and left. Rather than use any of the hotel lobby phones, I drove into town and found a pay booth in a local pharmacy. I dialed the four-digit number and at the second ring a man answered.

"Hello," he said in somewhat accented English.

I returned his greeting and asked if this was the Centura Travel Agency.

"Yes," he replied. "May I be of help?"

"I've a message for Mr. Kyle. Can you take it down now?"

His voice suddenly turned brisk, all business. "All of Mr. Kyle's messages have to be taken on tape. Is that agreeable with you, sir?"

I assured him it was okay, but that I wanted him to come back on once the message had been completed. A slight whirring sound followed, and then a recorded woman's voice came on, telling me to begin reading off my message when the signal tone sounded. I got out the sheet of paper, and at the sound of the bleep began reading off the message. When I finished I said that the message was completed, and after a short wait the man came back on.

"And now, sir?" he asked.

"I'll need confirmation on my message from Mr. Kyle some time this evening."

"Is it that urgent?"

"If it weren't I wouldn't ask."

I gave him my hotel phone number, a quick thank you and hung up.

When I got back to the car I lit a cigarette, then touched the flaming match to a corner of the message. When it flared up I let it drop into the dashboard ashtray.

I had no idea how the coded message would be routed, except that it would be relayed through some secret transmitter to the nearest NATO signal base. Confirmation would follow through some AXE logistic center in either Italy or Spain.

On the drive back to the hotel I couldn't help admiring the way Hawk had established AXE's intricate and highly successful lines of communication on a round-the-world basis. Even in Yugoslavia, a third-world country with Soviet ties, he had managed to keep a toe in the door. Somehow, someway, the proper connections had been worked out and pieced together—another link in AXE's almost endless, humming chain of command.

When I returned to my hotel room I called room service and ordered a sandwich, a carafe of coffee and a double shot of scotch. Ten minutes later the bellhop arrived with the tray.

I wolfed the sandwich down, but spent more time on the drink. Coffee came last, between puffs on a cigarette. After grinding out the cigarette, I got the plastic wrapped bundle from under the bed, untied it, and got to work on the Thompson submachinegun first.

I stripped it down carefully and oiled each part before reassembling it. I also checked the ammo clips, snapping them in and out to make sure of their fit. I also checked the Very pistol, the bullhorn and gave Wilhelmina, my small Luger, a thorough oiling. My final bit of preperation was to hone a fine cutting edge on Hugo.

At around 8:30 the Centura Travel Agency telephoned me as promised. It was the same guy I had spoken to that afternoon.

"Mr. Kyle has confirmed your booking," he said. "It will be held on a stand-by basis as requested for the next three days."

I thanked him, and when he clicked off I gave a little sigh of relief. It meant that my coded message had been received and approved, and that proper action would be taken by those on the other end.

I finished off what coffee was left in the carafe and lit another cigarette. There was still time to drop by Maya's, and I had to apply the brakes to keep myself from driving out to her place. But I held back. I didn't even call because I thought speaking to her would weaken my resolve. I hate goodbyes, but if I brought things off I'd be back. It was a promise I fully intended to keep, depending on events.

An hour later I went downstairs to the bar for a nightcap. It was a quiet scene. A couple sat in a corner booth, holding hands, with eyes only for themselves. A middle-aged man wearing thick-lensed glasses looked up when I entered, then went back to reading his newspaper. I ordered bourbon, but the bartender apologized for being out of it. American whiskey was hard to come by. I settled for another scotch.

I nursed the drink, recalling what Biro had told me about the prevelance of spies who operated under many covers. Was the bartender one of them? The couple? The man reading the newspaper? I shrugged, got up and left a fifty-dinar note alongside my empty glass. The couple paid no attention, and the guy with the thick-lenses remained buried in his newspaper.

Frankly, I believed he'd have trouble seeing me even if I stepped up and breathed in his face.

When I returned to my room I relocked the door and was between the sheets in less than ten minutes. It took even less time to fall asleep.

CHAPTER 14

The following morning I got off to an early start. By 7:00 I had paid my hotel bill and had carried the plastic-wrapped bundle out to the Fiat and had managed to cram it into the luggage section, along with the backpack and other camping gear. After locking up, I returned to the hotel's coffee shop for a quick breakfast of eggs, toast and coffee. I also had some sandwiches made up, and told the waitress to fill both of my thermos bottles with black coffee. At a little past eight I was on my way.

I drove slowly, under 60 kilometers, my eyes flicking from time to time to the rearview mirror. Traffic was brisk, and I'd occasionally pull over to let an oncoming car go by, but things looked okay.

At one point I simply relaxed. By now the whole strip of road had become quite familiar to me, and it was a little after nine when I arrived in Cavtat.

Minutes later I pulled up alongside the jetty and gave the horn a couple of bleeps. By the time I got out, the old man who had rented me the boat appeared in the shack's doorway.

He recognized me immediately and waved. *"Kako ste,"* everything was ready to go.

I let him carry some of the camping gear on board, but I managed the plastic bundle myself. When everything was stashed away inside the small cabin under the flybridge, I went back to the Fiat. I checked the front, rear and luggage compartments very thoroughly, just to be sure I hadn't left anything behind that could be traceable to me—including the butts in the ashtray.

When I finished, I drove the Fiat behind the small tool shed that stood alongside the jetty and parked it in the spot the old man had said I could use. I removed the keys, and before boarding the boat I turned them over to the old man.

"Sve najbolje," he grinned. *"Cuvajte se."* Good luck, and keep well.

"Mnogo vam hvala," I called back. Thanks for everything.

Moments later I hit the ignition switches and the engines came alive. The old man waved, and I waved back. A light breeze sprang up as I headed out to sea. I was on my way.

About a mile or so out, I swung her around and headed due north, my course directly parallel to the rocky shoreline. The day was mild, the unclouded sky a brilliant shade of blue. Occasionally, a sailboat scudded by, and once or twice a larger pleasure craft came up from behind, overtaking me and then moving ahead, its pounding engine churning the blue water into a foaming wake.

It wasn't quite noon when the soaring cliff with Korla's castle loomed off the starboard bow. I backed off on the engines and began heading in for shore, keeping an eye open for the small cove I had marked off on the map two days before. Minutes later I spotted it and spun the wheel hard to port. When I entered the cove I cut the engines to idling speed and drifted in to shore. A few minutes later a light scraping sound vibrated through the hull and I switched off the power. The stern swung left, thumping gently against the marshy bank. I hauled out the small anchor and dropped it over the side. So far so good.

I was in no great rush, so I went about my work carefully. The first thing I did was to get the weapon bundle out of the cabin, and the backpack. I untied the plastic sheeting and made a smaller bundle of the Thompson, the ammo clips, the bullhorn and the smoke grenades. I wrapped all of these together in one of the plastic sheets and strapped it in place on the backpack. I then tucked the Very pistol and the box of flares in a small storage compartment under the prow. The last item was the coil of nylon rope, and I was able to stuff this easily inside my jacket pocket. There was nothing about the backpack's appearance to give away what was inside the bulky bundle.

Satisfied, I got out the sandwiches and the coffee. While I ate, I switched on the boat's short-wave receiver. Within seconds I picked up a broadcast from the Italian mainland. It was a quartet, and when the music stopped the announcer gave the call letters of a Bari station. A brief Italian newscast followed, then more music. It was a Mozart piece and I listened for a while, but not intently. I was thinking ahead.

In about three hours I'd have to leave. Suddenly, it was all coming together. The final countdown had been long in coming, but it had finally begun. The mission's point-of-no-return had been reached. There could be no going back.

I snapped off the radio and stretched out on the deck. The only sounds were the gentle slaps of small waves against the resonant hull. I set my inner clock ahead for about two hours and quickly dropped off to sleep.

I awoke at precisely 3:30. Some clouds had

gathered along the western horizon, but the sky overhead was still a brilliant blue. I poured the last of the coffee from the first thermos and lit up a cigarette. Unseen birds chirped and scolded within the depths of the swaying marsh weeds. At intervals a frog let out a throaty croak. Beyond the weeds, where the embankment rose at a fairly steep angle, came the whine of tires as cars swept by on the highway some thirty yards off.

After I killed another fifteen minutes I buckled on the backpack and slipped the remaining sandwich inside my jacket pocket along with the boat's ignition keys. Seconds later I stepped ashore. The shoulder-high weeds crackled and snapped as I pushed my way through, and from time to time my boots sunk noisily into the muddy earth.

I reached the embankment and scrambled up. At the top, I turned and looked back in the direction of the boat. The broad sweep of weeds hid it almost entirely from view. So far so good. Turning, I moved out through the high grass. From this point the highway was less than twenty yards off, and I ducked at the sound of an approaching car. I could just make it out through the grass as it whizzed by. Moving in a crouch, I quickly covered the remaining distance, stepped over the guard rail and onto the highway.

I headed due north. Up ahead, the highway flowed into an S-curve and I counted off the paces as I went. The distance from where I started out, to the beginning of the curve, came to about two-tenths of a mile. I made a mental note of this.

I had already gauged the distance from the cove where I had anchored the boat, to Korla's castle, to be around three nautical miles, but I figured it would run closer to four miles by way of the highway. I maintained a good pace, about 120 steps to the minute, and it was approximately three-quarters of an hour later when I saw the castle high above the tree line to my left. At this point I crossed over to the other side of the highway, stepped over the guard rail and entered the flanking woods. About ten or so yards in I came across a small clearing. I unbuckled the backpack, balancing it against the trunk of a tree.

I checked my watch. It wasn't quite five. I was a bit ahead of my schedule, which was just as well. There was no chance of my being seen from the highway, so I took out a cigarette. The sun was well over to the left, moving toward the horizon. The light in the woods was dimming fast. About thirty minutes later I buckled on the backpack and headed back for the highway.

When I got there, dusk was already settling in. The sun had dipped below a bank of lavender clouds. I had timed it just about right. A few early stars showed in the northern sky and much of the landscape was already shrouded in shadows. Stepping over the guard rail, I started up the highway, heading north. I kept close to the shoulder and maintained a good hiking stride. About a half-hour later, as the night darkened, the dark bulk of the cliff loomed high above the tree line to my right. Ten minutes later I breezed right by the castle which was already cloaked in darkness.

When I had continued down the road for about another quarter-of-a-mile, I quickly crossed the road and began retracing my steps.

I soon found what I wanted, a row of tangled bushes. Ducking behind them, I squatted down behind the thick cover. My position gave me fairly good view of the castle's facade, with the front gates and the winding gravel road leading down to the highway. It was all I needed. I got out my binoculars and gave it a careful going over. It looked no different than it had the other days. No sign of life disturbed its tomb-like appearance and I settled down to wait.

Along the western horizon the sky still glowed where the sun had set, and I watched it fade gradually, like the house lights in a theater before the curtain goes up.

Minutes later the last of the light was gone. I checked my watch. The luminous hands read 6:20. My impatience began to grow. A great deal depended on the next few minutes. At 6:25 I went back to the binoculars. I focused them on the castle's front gates, straining to catch a glimpse of the limousine's headlights. Six-thirty came and went. Nothing happened. I wiped the sweat from my forehead. Another five minutes dragged by. Still nothing.

I cursed under my breath. For four nights running, Korla had turned up with clock-like regularity. Why the switch, I wondered. Suddenly, I began to feel edgy. Had Korla caught wind of my spying? It was a possibility.

I weighed the thought, wondering where I might have slipped up. There were too many imponderables to be able to pinpoint any one thing in particular. There was also the possibility that Korla may have had me under surveillance without my suspecting it. If so, I could have been setting myself up without knowing it. I glanced around. Nothing stirred. I strained my hearing, but other than a slight, stirring breeze, heard nothing. I rechecked my watch—6:52.

Korla had given me six days to come up with the money and a payoff plan, and this was the fifth. By tomorrow I could run out of time and the picture could be unalterably changed. I had set everything on tonight. Everything.

I squirmed around on my heels. Another three, four minutes dragged by. I pressed the binoculars to my eyes and came close to letting out a whoop. Two circles of light gleamed brightly, high up along the cliff. Slowly they began their descent. I let the glasses go slack on the cord and let out a sigh of relief. Gradually, the limo came down the long, winding driveway. At the point where it met the highway it paused briefly, then swung left, heading north as usual for Dubrovnik. As it slid past my cover, I peered from between the bushes and caught a quick glimpse of Korla's huge bulk hunched up on the back seat.

"About time, you fat bastard," I grinned. I was feeling a hell of a lot better.

When the taillights winked off in the distant gloom, I left my cover. Keeping close to the bushes I followed the highway to the point where it was joined by the gravel road that led up to the castle. They formed a kind of fork, with the main highway continuing south while the graveled road branched off, breaking away into a sweeping curve on its upward climb.

Satisfied, I retraced my steps to a point about sixty feet below the fork. A patch of thick, waist-high grass bordered the shoulder, dense enough to offer reasonable cover, but with enough breaks in between to observe cars coming in either direction. I moved into the grass, slipped off the backpack and squatted down. I untied the bulky bundle that contained the military hardware and removed the Thompson machinegun. I thumbed it on safety and rammed in one of the ammo clips. I then slipped the remaining three clips inside my right jacket pocket, along with the coil of nylon rope. There was also the bullhorn and the smoke grenades, and I set them aside on one of the plastic sheets.

I placed the Thompson on the ground beside me. The countdown was on at last. Meanwhile, I made no point of thinking too far ahead. Even the best of plans have a way of taking unexpected turns, and what I had in mind could hardly be called a sure thing. It was an outside shot, the kind of gambling odds that would make Hawk fume. He would have labeled it "harebrained—sheer lunacy." And he would have been right. But under the circumstances it was the best I could come up with. It was as simple as that.

The first couple of hours seemed to last forever. I watched the stars come out, listened to the cars as they drove by my position. By ten the traffic had slowed down, with only one or two cars or an occasional truck lumbering by over a span of ten or fifteen minutes. By eleven they were coming by even less frequently.

I watched a late, almost full moon come up, rising slowly from beyond a rim of distant hills like a giant, silver balloon. Gradually, it began its westward drift, appearing and disappearing between banks of dark clouds.

Somewhere along the way I finished off the last sandwich and poured some coffee from the second thermos. I followed this with another cigarette, and when I ground out the butt I checked my watch. It was 12:08. On the other nights when I had kept watch, Korla had returned around one, give or take five minutes. This left around forty-five minutes to run through my final preparations.

First, I rechecked the Thompson, making certain the clip was firmly in place. Next, I tested the bullhorn, activating the on-off switch and blowing gently into the mouthpiece. It made a slight crackling sound that indicated it was operative. The smoke grenades came last. I put one of them alongside the bullhorn, and slipped the other two inside my left jacket pocket.

By now road traffic had fallen off to a trickle and I was depending heavily on this. At this point no vehicle had passed in either direction for almost twenty minutes. At around 12:30 I fiddled with the Thompson's gunsling, adjusting it to a position that felt comfortable when I slipped it over my left shoulder. At about 12:40 the lights of an approaching car, heading south in my direction, blazed brilliantly as it topped the rise in the road. I tensed momentarily, but it roared right by, blue exhaust trailing in its wake. For the next ten minutes, no further cars appeared.

It was a bit past 12:50 when the moon, with almost perfect timing, slipped out from behind a cloud cover. Pale, silvery light illuminated the highway as I focused my attention north in the direction from which Korla would be coming. It wasn't more than a few seconds later when I heard the faint whine of approaching tires. I reached down with my right hand and picked up the smoke grenade. I was well within the thick patch of grass, only a bit of my head poking out. The sound grew louder. The glow of headlamps appeared over the rise. There was no mistaking the black limo as it began slowing down, edging toward the shoulder to pick up the gravel road that led up to the castle.

I waited until it was about ten yards away before pinning the grenade. It made a slight popping sound, and I made my underhand toss in advance of the oncoming car. It landed on the sandy shoulder and went into a spluttering spin. There was a brief, blue-white flash, a muffled *swoosh* and suddenly a mushrooming cloud of dense smoke billowed skyward.

Brakes screeching, the limo slid past my position, jerking to a halt. A split second later the driver's door burst open and the chauffeur leaped out. He leaped around to the front end of the car, running toward the smoking column for a moment before pulling up short.

I slipped the Thompson off my shoulder, ducked into a crouch and sped toward him. His back was to me, his knees bent, as though he were trying to look under the cloud to see what was causing it. I spun the Thompson around, gripping it by the barrel like a baseball bat. He heard me coming, but before he could straighten up I drove the gun's solid wood stock smack up between his crotch. He let out an anguished cry, his hands clutching at his groin as he fell. He hit the ground face down, making wet, grunting sounds as his stomach emptied.

Pivoting, I raced back to the limo and yanked open the rear door. I dragged Korla out, slamming his back hard against the door. His puffy eyes had a dazed, bewildered look. For a second or two he just stared, and then recognition hit him.

"*Carter!*" he gasped.

I thumbed the Thompson off safety and slipped the muzzle under his trembling, flabby chin.

"*Move!*" I snapped.

I pushed him toward the front of the car and he stumbled and came close to falling. I grabbed him by the jacket, swung his bulk around and propped him up against the front fender. Some of the initial bewilderment was gone now. His control was coming back, so I prodded the Thompson's barrel against his ribs, to keep him running scared.

Sweat beaded his upper lip and dripped from the corners of his slack mouth. He swallowed, choking on his saliva. "What's going on?" he blurted. "*W—what?*"

I slapped the engine hood with my palm. "Up you go, Korla. On the double."

He shook his head with disbelief. "*N—no.*"

I punched the Thompson's stock into his gut, just hard enough to knock him off balance. He toppled back, arms flapping. I used my shoulder, ramming it into his chest and shoved him up and over the fender and onto the hood. He lay there on his back, panting, the top of his head just below the windshield. He was really sweating rivers now. I slung the Thompson over my shoulder, dipped into my jacket pocket and came up with the coil of nylon rope.

A man stretched out on his back is literally helpless, and that's the way I wanted Korla. I wanted him helpless and terrified, and I was getting it both ways. Now I intended to add the element of shock and sap what remaining will was left and make him totally submissive to my demands.

"Do as you're told," I warned him, "and you might go on living. Try anything and I'll crack your skull like an eggshell."

I quickly threw a coil of rope around his right ankle, giving it a couple of turns and yanking it tight. He let out a whimpering cry, but when I made a move for the Thompson he choked it off. I threw a second loop around the same ankle and threaded the free end of the rope down between the bumper. I gave it a couple of turns around the bumper guard, threaded the end back up again and then looped it a couple of times around his left ankle.

The rest went quickly. I brought the rope down again, gave it a couple of more turns around the bumper, then up across Korla's chest and then another loop around his right wrist. I knotted it tightly and then tied what was left of the rope to the car's right, sideview mirror. This left Korla spread-eagled, but with his left hand free—which was precisely what I wanted.

Turning, I darted back toward the patch of grass where I had left the bullhorn. About halfway there I heard a light shuffling sound. I spun toward it. The chauffeur had partially recovered and was trying to pull himself up. When I closed in, he turned, his hand fumbling inside his tunic. He came up with a snub-nosed automatic, but his hand wobbled badly. I whacked him across the knuckles with the flat side of the Thompson's stock and the gun went spinning off into the roadside bushes. Cursing, he began tottering to his feet. I jabbed the stock through a short arc and the steel butt plate caught him under the chin. There was a dry, snapping sound and he spilled over on his back.

I waited a few seconds, but he didn't budge. Turning, I ran back to the patch of grass, scooped up the bullhorn and hustled back to Korla. His eyes bulged with terror as I slipped the Thompson off my shoulder. When I touched the muzzle to his left ear I could feel his flesh quiver.

"Okay, Korla," I said flatly. "You listen carefully because I'm only going to say it once. In a few minutes you're going to get the chance to save your fat hide. What you're going to do is to tell your goons to bring Salobin out, and he'd better be in good shape. Now if you do exactly as you're told, I promise I'll cut you loose later on. But remember, you're a fat, juicy target.

Try any tricks, get your men to open fire and I'll blow the top of your head off right through the windshield."

I backhanded him twice across the face to make sure the message had sunk through.

"You understand?"

"What makes you so sure Salobin is here?" he gasped.

I couldn't help grinning. "Then you'd better start praying. Because if Salobin isn't produced, you're about ten minutes away from becoming a corpse."

Darting around to the driver's side, I pulled open the door and slid in behind the wheel. I quickly lowered the driver's window down all the way and released the brake. The engine was in neutral, so I slipped the gear lever into drive, toed the accelerator and eased forward. The wind had carried away most of the smoke from the grenade as I eased over to the right and onto the graveled driveway that led up to the castle. I kept the big car down to a crawl, maneuvering it cautiously through the first two sweeping curves. The top of Korla's head blocked a portion of the windshield, but I could see well enough up ahead.

The castle was in almost total darkness, but when I had made it about halfway up, a light suddenly came on above the front gates. I braked to a quick halt, sucked in my breath and slapped my palm down hard on the horn.

A lot of things happened at once. Lights began showing behind windows, voices were raised. I kept leaning on the horn until a spotlight, high up on one of the turrets, stabbed my way. A second one joined in. The beams moved inward, stopping abruptly when they centered on the vehicle.

The sight of Korla, bound and squirming on the hood of his limo, must have shocked them out of their skulls. Tiny figures darted along the castle's upper walls. Shouts and yells floated across the air, and more lights kept popping on. For the moment I held the advantage, and I made my move. I snatched up the bull-horn, thumbed the switch on and passed it out the driver's window.

"Grab this," I yelled to Korla. "Better tell them to hold their fire."

He reacted instantly. His left hand flew back and I pressed the bullhorn into his sweating palm. A moment later his voice, choked up with fear, boomed out. "Don't shoot!" he shrieked in Croat. *"Don't shoot!"*

The shouting along the wall broke off instantly. Silence. I slipped the Thompson out the open window, laying the muzzle alongside Korla's head. "Tell them they have five minutes to bring Salobin out. Tell them if he isn't down here by then I'll blow your head off. And remember, I understand your language—so no tricks."

His hand trembled as he put the bullhorn to his mouth. For a few moments he made strange, slobber-ing sounds and then the words spilled out. He repeated the message almost word for word. They were to bring Salobin down immediately.

I prodded the Thompson's muzzle against his skull for added effect, and he really hit the panic button.

"Napred, napred!" he screamed. Hurry—hurry.

I eased back on the Thompson and checked my watch. When about three minutes had passed, I gave Korla another nudge with the muzzle.

"You've got two minutes left," I warned. "Better get them moving."

He let out a howl and began shrieking into the bull-horn. It helped. Less than a minute later the front gate swung open and two men hustled out supporting a frail, white-haired man between them. I gave Korla an-other nudge with the Thompson.

"Tell your men to go back inside. I want Salobin all by himself."

Korla continued to cooperate. His voice came close to cracking under the strain, but he repeated my in-structions exactly.

Within seconds, the two men withdrew behind the gate, leaving Salobin alone on the graveled roadway. For a while the old man seemed uncertain as to which way to go. He took a few steps forward. Stopped. Started up again. Then came to another halt.

I reached out the window, snatched the bullhorn from Korla's hand.

"Salobin," I called out. "I am a friend—an American. I am here to help you. Do you understand? I am here to help you. Start coming down."

Apparently his English was good enough to understand my message, because he suddenly broke into a wobbly run. Twice he came close to falling. I toed the accelerator and zoomed forward. When I pulled alongside him, I braked hard. Reaching back, I unlatched the rear door, swung it partly open. Gasping, he crawled in and I slammed the door shut behind him.

"Down," I yelled. "On the floor."

Reaching out the window, I rammed the bullhorn back into Korla's hand. "One more thing," I snapped. "Tell your men to stay right where they are. No one's to follow. If they come after us, Korla, you die."

I waited until he delivered the message, then shifted into reverse.

It was tricky backing the car down the winding driveway, but I wanted to keep Korla facing up front. As long as he was exposed, it would keep his men from opening fire. I managed the first winding curve, straightened out, and then backed into the second, the spinning rear wheels throwing up clouds of gravel. I kept checking the rear mirror. About twenty yards remained.

I called out to Salobin. "Be careful. Hold on tight."

"Da, da," he replied quickly.

I gunned the accelerator, spun through the final S-curve and came out on the highway. I cut hard right to get the front end pointing south. For a brief moment the limo's right side was exposed to possible fire, but with Korla fully exposed they held off. I slammed the car into drive, floored the pedal and took off like a shot.

I couldn't quite believe it yet. It had actually worked. In less than five minutes we'd be at the point where I had anchored the boat. A movement came from behind me. I glanced into the rear view mirror as Salobin's strained face popped into view. The lid of his left eye, the false one, drooped noticeably. I had the right man.

"W—who are you?" he stammered in accented English.

I laughed. "Superman, the mild-mannered reporter."

He shook his head dazedly. "I—I do not understand."

"It's all right," I said reassuringly. "I'm an American like I said. You're safe now, Salobin. Everything's going to be fine. But keep your head down."

"*Da,*" he said obediently, and popped out of sight.

I checked the rearview mirror. No lights showed from behind. Obviously, for the moment anyway, Korla's hysterical plea had kept his men in line. I let out a sigh of relief.

There was no joy in it for Korla. His bulk shifted under the rope, and his left hand was thrown across his face to ward off the slicing wind. He had gone through a hell of a lot, but I couldn't have cared less. Meanwhile, I was prepared to keep my word and cut the bastard loose once we reached the cove. How he'd manage from there would damn well be his problem, not mine.

Less than three minutes later I approached the sweeping curve I had paced off after leaving the boat. The cove would be right behind it, less than a tenth of a mile. As I roared out of the turn I began slowing down, coming to a screeching halt alongside the highway guard rail.

A split second later lots of things began to happen.

A pair of headlamps, dead ahead, suddenly blazed on. I ducked instinctively. A splatter of gunfire broke out. The windshield went first, filling the car with flying shards of glass. I glanced up. What was left of Korla's skull had been scattered with the glass. Blood sloshed thickly over the dashboard and down the wheel.

"OUT!" I yelled to Salobin. "*Out!*"

I grabbed the Thompson and flung open the passenger door. I slid out, falling to the ground as another volley burst out. I wormed forward toward the front right wheel, bringing up the Thompson. The headlamps were an easy target. I got off a quick burst and the lights went dark instantly.

Suddenly, two shadowy figures darted toward the limo. They were shouting to each other, and there was no mistaking the language—*Russian!* I squeezed off another burst. The lead man went down, clutching his chest. A second later the one behind tripped over his fallen companion. He recovered quickly, scrambling for his fallen weapon. I tilted the Thompson slightly and squeezed the trigger. His hands flew to his face and he fell forward across the first man's crumpled body. I didn't waste a second.

Scurrying back, I yanked the rear passenger door open. I reached in, grabbed Salobin's arm and pulled him out and down to the ground. I literally threw him over the low guard rail and then followed suit. I hit in a heap, my body spinning as I rolled down the slight incline. I ended up on my back, still clutching the Thompson. I heard footsteps. At first I couldn't see him, but then the moon slipped out from behind a cloud, flooding the scene with silvery light. He was at the guard rail, and one foot already over. I fired while still on my back, a quick raking burst while the recoil tore at my arms. His scream filled the night, and he dropped like a stone.

Sounds came from my left. I rolled to my knees.

Salobin crawled my way, breathing hard. I grabbed him under the left arm.

"Are you all right?"

He nodded shakily. *"Da,"* he whispered. "All right."

We were still some distance from the boat, but I wasn't ready to chance an open run for it. I glanced around and spotted a thick patch of marsh weeds up ahead. For the moment it offered the best protective cover. I tugged at Salobin's arm, pulling him shakily to his knees. I nodded toward the weeds.

"We can't stay here. There are others."

He nodded again. "I understand," he whispered back.

Taking a firm grip on his arm, I started forward. Twice his knees came close to buckling under him, and I tightened my grip. We were making more noise than I liked, but it couldn't be helped. We hit the weeds and I pulled him in after me. There were movements from behind, but they suddenly broke off. I yanked out the clip that was in the Thompson and rammed in a fresh one.

I had no way of knowing how many were out there, but they were Russians. That much I did know. Somehow, some way, they had gotten on to me and had planned the ambush. But they wouldn't wait long. I was convinced of that. It was only a matter of minutes before they'd try again. So far I had managed to pick off a few, but if they decided to rush me, my back would be up the old wall.

A few more seconds slid by. Somewhere within the dense marsh weeds a frog croaked. Another joined in. The moon slipped behind another cloud and the night closed in like a tightening noose.

I nudged Salobin. "We've got to move now while we have the chance. I have a boat waiting, but we've got a bit more to go. We must try and get to it. Do you understand?"

"I understand," he said gently.

I took his arm again, waited, our heads just below the tops of the wafted marsh weeds.

"Now," I whispered.

I used the barrel of the Thompson to part the weeds as we made our slow, cautious advance. Every so often I stopped to listen. The wind blowing off the sea stirred the dry weeds and they brushed against each other noisily. Other sounds came from behind, slight crackling movements, but too vague to distinguish clearly.

At the point where the marsh weeds began to thin out, I came to another halt. The cove lay before us, across a short span of open beach. I distinctly heard the light slap of waves. Moments later I spotted the boat's silhouette, a dark shadow among darker shadows. We would have to make a break for it and take our chances. There was no other way. I listened. The crackling sounds from behind had increased. I gripped Salobin's arm.

"We'll have to run. Will you try?"

"I will try," he murmured.

I sucked in my breath. *"Now!"*

We were off and running.

About halfway there the shots broke out from behind. Sand kicked up at our heels. I slammed Salobin to the ground, dropped to one knee and pivoted around. They were breaking through the cover of the weeds. There seemed to be four of them, possibly five. The ambush must have involved two cars, perhaps as many as three. Their fire fell short, kicking up spurts of loose sand. I squeezed off a sweeping burst. Two men fell.

I dipped inside my pocket and came up with one of the smoke grenades. I pinned it and made my toss. It landed about a half-dozen yards in front of them. It flashed blue-white, detonated thuddingly. They let out a few surprised shouts, darting back as the thick smoke billowed into the air. Just to be sure, I raked the cloud with another burst, then grabbed Salobin under the armpit and hauled him to his feet.

I sprinted for the boat, dragging Salobin as best I could. The distance closed, but when we were almost there, a figure popped up in the prow. Orange flame tongued the air. I dropped Salobin and fired the Thompson from my hip. His hands jerked straight up over his head. He tottered, fell forward, hit the railing and then hung there, his arms dangling stiffly over the side.

I carried Salobin the remaining distance, propped him against the boat and told him to hang on. Grabbing the dead man by the arm, I yanked hard. He toppled over the rail, falling heavily to the beach. Darting back to Salobin, I tossed him on deck, then ran around to the stern. Pulling up the anchor, I heaved it aboard and scrambled to the deck.

While I raced for the wheel, I fumbled in my pocket for the ignition keys. I glanced back. Two of the Russians had managed to find their way through the billowing smoke screen. I got off another burst and drove them back. Seconds later I hit the ignition and the twin engines came alive.

Reaching inside my jacket pocket I came up with the last smoke grenade. I yanked the pin and tossed it over the stern and onto the beach. It detonated on impact. I fed the engines and a light scraping sound followed as the hull broke loose from the sandy bottom. With a leap, the boat surged forward.

Once I cleared the cove, I headed straight out for sea. When we were beyond the cove I looked back over my shoulder. The spreading smoke screen had blanketed the beach, cutting off any chance of our being seen. Sporadic gunfire broke out somewhere behind us, but they didn't even come close. The shots grew fainter and then stopped altogether. Gradually, I felt the muscles along my shoulders relax.

"How are you?" I called out to Salobin.

He lay huddled up toward the prow, a small pathetic bundle. "My leg," he murmured. "It pains . . ."

With all the running and falling, he'd have to be bruised. "I'll have a look at it," I reassured him. "But we'd better get a little further out to sea first."

I gunned the engines and the prow rose gracefully out of the water, throwing up twin curtains of shooting spray. The only thing that really bothered me now was how the Russians had gotten on to me. Biro came to mind immediately. He was the only one to have had precise knowledge as to my exact whereabouts. It was a depressing thought. I shook my head wearily. An old war buddy of Hawk, and a one time OSS man, besides. It seemed incredible, but it would have to be dealt with at the proper time. Meanwhile, it was first things first.

I eased back on the throttle all the way. When we came to a gentle, bobbing halt I switched off the engines and went forward to take a look at Salobin's leg. The problem was with his left ankle. He had either wrenched it while running, or when I had thrown him to the ground. From what I could see and feel, it was badly swollen, but it didn't seem like a break. Meanwhile, there was little I could do for him at the moment, other than assure him that help was on the way.

As carefully as I could, I explained that a couple of days earlier I had dispatched a coded message to the American headquarters of an Italian based NATO command station, and that I received prompt confirmation that a rescue vessel would be dispatched at the proper time.

"They should be heading our way right about now," I continued. "My message included the location we'd be in, and the approximate time to expect us." I gave his arm a gentle squeeze. "You've been through the worst of it. It won't be long now."

The lid of his false, left eye tugged slightly as he smiled. "You are a very brave man to do all of this for a stranger." He put his hand over mine. "I trust you, and I thank you . . ."

I gave his arm another pat and flipped open the storage compartment where I had put the Very pistol and the flares. I got them out, placed the pistol on the deck alongside me and tore open the top flap of the flare carton. I took out one of the shells and was about to load the pistol when the cabin door behind me clicked sharply. I spun around as the shadowy figure emerged.

Recognition came instantly.

"*Maya!*"

Her slender hand gripping the snub-nosed automatic didn't waver.

"Turn around, Nick," she said curtly. "Put your hands behind your head."

The shock waves were still hitting me as I turned slowly, doing exactly as she said. A moment later the muzzle of her automatic touched the base of my spine. Her left hand came around, dipped inside my jacket. She neatly removed Wilhelmina from my shoulder holster and stepped back.

"You can turn now."

Her eyes met mine unblinkingly. She stood with her back to the boat's rail, her weapon pointed directly at my chest.

I was still dazed out of my head. "It was *you*," I finally whispered. "You led them to me. You're one of them."

She nodded. "I'm a member of the KGB—satellite division."

I felt my jaw go slack. "So you knew all about me. Who I was all along."

She shook her head. "Not really. It was a matter of unusual coincidences, things coming together at the right time. My working for Biro was purely routine. I was advised by my superiors to apply for the position. Planting agents inside an American organization is typical procedure for our division. Frequently, it provides useful information, but I was just another plant until you unexpectedly turned up."

She paused, and for a moment her eyes softened. "That first day when we met and had dinner with Biro and then you took me back to my cottage. The phone was ringing when we got there. Remember? When I answered, it was one of my superiors. They already knew all about you. I was given my special orders, and I followed them as best I could."

I forced myself to go on talking. I was fighting for time. "You did exceptionally well tracing me to the boat. How?"

She shrugged. For a moment I thought she was going to let the question slide by.

"It took a while," she continued. "Remember the last time you came to my cottage, when you spent the night? In the morning I brought you your shaving equipment from your car, but I did something else, too. I planted a magnetic bug under the fender of your Fiat, a small but efficient transmitter. The signals allowed us to follow your movements at a safe distance. We were able to trail you to Cavtat where you picked up your boat, but when we finally arrived at the marina, and located the parked Fiat, you were already on your way."

"And so you got the old man to talk."

She gave another shrug. "He proved difficult at first, but there are ways of persuading people to do what is best for them."

"And eventually you located the cove with the boat . . ."

"Eventually," she echoed flatly. "But the important thing at that moment was that we were convinced that you had come up with some plan of freeing Salobin from his kidnappers, although we didn't know who they were or where they held him. Of course, not long after you had arrived in Beirut, the KGB knew of your presence and your probable mission. At first it was planned to kill you, and, as you well know, attempts were made. But at one point the plan was changed. It was agreed that if you succeeded in freeing Salobin, you would be doing our work for us. So it made simple sense to wait; give you a free hand to effect your plan."

"And so the ambush was planned."

"Exactly," she replied. "But the good luck turned bad. Locating the cove with your boat proved difficult. There must be at least fifty coves between here and Cavtat, and we kept missing yours. We searched for hours, and when night came it made it even more difficult. Finally we found it, but only minutes before you turned up. When the shooting broke out and you were able to get away, another man and myself ran back to the boat. We intended to sabotage it, but suddenly you were there on the beach with Salobin. When you shot the man who was with me, there was no longer time . . ."

"And so you hid in the cabin," I said slowly. "You waited. And now, Maya. What happens now? Are you telling me to hand Salobin over to you?"

"It is much too late for that," she snapped back. "I regret what has to be done. I wish we had met differently. But you know the rules that govern our lives—our mission always comes first."

She nodded toward Salobin who lay huddled in the prow. "The vital scientific knowledge this man possesses must never fall into the hands of the United States or any other power. We were given only one order; *kill Salobin on sight*."

Wheeling suddenly, she fired point blank at the old man. I heard his cry of pain and lunged. Spinning toward me, she fired again. Pain stabbed my left arm. I reeled back, and she turned again toward Salobin. I flicked my right arm and Hugo snapped into my waiting palm. I made an underhanded throw. It thudded in below her left breast. Her violet eyes widened with pain and surprise. The smoking gun slid from her hand. Tottering, she managed to tug the knife free. As it clattered to the deck, a long, low wave swept against the boat's hull, tilting it at a sharp angle. She was already off balance when I raced for her. She fell back, struck the rail and went over. I caught a fleeting glimpse of her body borne forward along the crest of the sweeping wave. She lay on her back, only her pale, oval face glowing faintly against the inky, black water. A moment later she slid into the trough and the wave foamed over her.

"*Maya,*" I whispered.

Yellow moonlight dappled the spot where I had seen her last. She was gone ...

What followed was purely a series of mechanical movements. Somehow, I managed to get to Salobin's side. He was unconscious. I checked his pulse and the faint beat was irregular. Blood drenched his chest. I started up the engines, only faintly aware of the pain in my left arm. My major concern at the moment was Salobin. Would he die? There was nothing more I could do but head west, out to sea.

Less than five minutes later I heard the throb of engines moving my way. I switched off the diesels. The throbbing beat grew louder. Lights suddenly blinked ahead, off the starboard prow. I went forward, found the Very pistol where I had laid it and rammed a shell into the wide muzzle. I pointed it straight up and squeezed the trigger. It slashed into the dark sky, trailing sparks like a rocket. About 200 feet up it detonated, turning the night momentarily into day.

It wasn't much later when the power launch loomed into view. Moments later the launch and its four-man crew had drawn alongside. A youthful, life-jacketed officer sprang aboard.

He threw a crisp salute. "Lt. Walters, NATO division, United States Navy. May I be of assistance, sir?"

I pointed to Salobin. "Get him abroad. He needs medical attention desperately."

When they had transferred Salobin to the launch, I collected my few pieces of gear. I found Wilhelmina where Maya had dropped it, and Hugo a few feet away. I dropped my hankerchief over the blood stained blade and carefully slipped it inside my pocket.

A moment later Lt. Walters joined me. Suddenly he spotted my injured arm. "It looks as if you'll be needing some care too, sir." He paused and frowned. "If you'll excuse me," he said carefully, "are there just the two of you. I mean, only you and the old man?"

I knew what was bothering him, but I wasn't going to clear it up. "That's right, Lieutenant," I said quietly. "Just the two of us."

His frown deepened. "But if you and the old man have been shot, it would mean—" He broke off awkwardly. "Are you ready to leave, sir?"

"Ready," I replied.

We boarded the launch and were on our way.

CHAPTER 15

Commander Horace Fuller, the cruiser's captain, was enormously helpful and cooperative. Within moments after we came aboard, he had Salobin rushed to the ship's sick bay, and ordered a medical corpsman to look after my arm. With the flesh wound cauterized and neatly bandaaged, I sat in Fuller's cabin while he poured a generous amount of scotch into a tall glass.

"My orders," he explained, "were to check these waters for three consecutive nights, starting with tonight, and to pick up an American and anyone else who may happen to be with him. I was also told not to ask questions, make no official record of your presence in the log, and to offer all possible assistance you might request."

He smiled as I tossed off the drink, but I refused his offer for a refill. I was worried about Salobin, right down to my toes. When I expressed my feelings, Fuller sympathized.

"He's not in good shape," Fuller readily admitted,

"and his age is working against him. But we're heading for the Italian mainland at top speed, and there's a first class hospital with NATO facilities in Bari. Meanwhile, he's getting the best medical care under the circumstances. Lt. Baker is young, but a first rate doctor. I've told him that you wanted to see your companion as soon as possible, and he was to report immediately if there was any change in his condition, up or down."

A split second later, as though on cue, the intercom buzzed. Fuller slipped the receiver off its hook and clamped it to his ear. I saw the muscles in his jaw tense. He dropped the receiver back on the hook.

"Not good," he said. "He's slipping. I suppose you want to see him."

I was standing when Fuller got back on the intercom. "Send someone to the captain's cabin immediately," he snapped. "Make this fast."

Less than a minute later we heard quick footsteps, followed by the knock on the door. Fuller opened, addressed the tall, youthful sailor. "Take this man to the sick bay, and hurry."

I stepped into the corridor.

"Good luck," Fuller called after me.

There was a companionway at the end of the corridor and we took it down. From here we followed a narrow passageway and turned left. At the third door to our right, the young sailor stopped. He opened the door and stepped aside. I entered, and a young lieutenant came toward me.

"Lt. Baker?"

"Yes," he replied. "He's in here."

He led the way into a small, private cabin off the main sick bay. Salobin's face was whiter than the pillow case. His right eye was slitted almost shut, and the lid of the false left eye was totally closed. A stand to the left of the bed piped an intravenous flow of blood plasma into his left arm.

"Has he recovered consciousness at any time?" I asked.

Baker shook his head. "And he may not. The bullet severed his spinal cord on the way out. He's totally paralyzed from the hips down. I'd go ahead with surgery, try to pinch off some of the severed blood vessels, but he'd go right into cardiac arrest."

"How's the blood pressure?"

"Awful. And the cardiogram's even worse. Scarcely any peaks. Almost a straight line."

He glanced at the plastic plasma container. "That's the second pint. But there's no meaningful response. He's losing more through internal bleeding than what's coming in."

He leaned across the raised hospital bed and put his stethescope to Salobin's chest. When he straightened up he gave his head another shake. "All I'm getting is a whisper. It can happen at any time."

"I want to stay with him," I said. "Just in case he does come around."

Baker nodded. "I'll be outside. Call if you want me."

He left the room, closing the door silently behind him.

I sat down in the chair alongside the bed, stared at Salobin's drawn face, at the withered cheeks drained of all color. I experienced a deep sense of helplessness. So much had happened and so many had died. The last was Maya, and soon it would be Salobin's turn.

The mission, of course, had failed, and though this was something that could always happen, I blamed myself completely. And Maya, whom I had trusted completely had been my undoing. In one blinding flash her bullet had turned what could have been success into total failure.

But I felt no anger toward her. She had done her job, much the same as I would, and she had done it well. Her bravery and courage were implicit. I recalled the afternoon we had driven to the mountain inn, when the hit man in the Porsche had come up from behind. They had set her up to get at me, and if we had died together the KGB wouldn't have cared less. She must have realized this later, but good soldier that she was, she remained loyal to her beliefs and training, despite the fact that her own life had hung in the balance.

But all at once a movement from the bed snapped me back to the present. Salobin's right hand had moved slightly. A moment later his right eye fluttered open. I leaned over him. Recognition showed. His lips moved. He was trying to say something. I leaned closer. All I could hear were choked, inaudible whispers.

"Louder," I pleaded. *"Louder!"*

Then I heard it, but very faintly. *"I . . . I,"* as though he were trying to make some kind of statement.

I leaned closer still. *" 'I',* what?" I asked. *"What?"*

His lips twitched and blood-flecked saliva oozed from the corners of his mouth. He gagged, and choked, but he was beyond speech. He struggled, raising his right hand shakily and began tracing a trembling finger in the air, as though he were trying to draw something.

I reached inside my pocket, snatched out my pad and ballpoint pen. I quickly raised the bed to an upright position and managed to get the pen between his trembling fingers. Flipping open the pad, I slid it underneath and placed my hand around his to keep the pen from slipping between his fingers. His hand moved awkwardly within mine as he guided the pen. Painfully, slowly, he traced out a scrawled, lopsided circle. He paused, and then, with a final effort, he placed a dot in the center.

The pen slid free and his hand stiffened in mine. He coughed. Blood welled from his mouth and a harsh rattling rose from his throat. I slid my arm around his frail shoulders. Like a light being dimmed, his good right eye clouded over. Gently, I eased his head against the pillow and quickly lowered the bed.

When I opened the door, Lt. Baker joined me instantly. He moved quickly to Salobin's side, pressed his stethescope to Salobin's chest. In a moment he straightened.

"He's dead," he sighed. "I'll notify Captain Fuller." He paused at the door. "Will you be coming, sir?"

"In a minute."

When he left I stared at the sheet of paper with the crude circle Salobin had scrawled. I groped at its meaning. He had desperately tried to get some message through. But *what?* A circle and a dot in its center. My thoughts whirled. It made no sense. But all at once I was remembering. When Salobin had said "I" twice, he may not have been referring to himself. Suddenly it struck me. Could the circle and dot he had drawn mean *eye?*

Gently, I raised the lid of his false, left eye. I pressed gently against it and the plastic eyeball popped free. Carefully, I plucked it out. I examined it under the bedside lamp. A thin, inscribed slit circled the circumference. I ran the edge of my fingernail along the slit and it sprang open on a tiny, inner hinge. I gasped. Nested inside the hollow sphere was a tightly rolled celluloid coil. I tapped it into my palm, unrolled it. It was approximately an eight-inch strip of microfilm, no more than an eighth-of-an-inch in width.

I pocketed it quickly. Snapping the plastic eye shut, I carefully pressed it back into the gaping eye socket. Gently, I drew the lid over it and did the same for the right eye. At the door, I looked back. Death had restored a measure of tranquillity to the pallid face.

I stepped out, closed the door gently behind me.

CHAPTER 16

I sat in Hawk's office, my written report lying on his cluttered desk. I had flown out of Rome the day before and wrote most of the report while over the Atlantic dropping it off along with the strip of microfilm late the previous night. I knew the film had been taken away for immediate analysis, and I was anxious to hear the verdict. Hawk was fully aware of this, but he was taking his own sweet time in getting around to it.

Leaning back in his creaky, swivil chair, he lit up an inch of dead cigar. He sucked in, then blew out a reeking cloud of smoke. He picked up my report, let it drop and shook his head ruefully.

"Dammit, N3," he said, "there are times you can make a grown man cry."

His back was up about something, and I decided to bring things to a head.

"Is it the microfilm, sir? Is it all that bad?"

"*Bad!*" he shot back. "Who said anything about it

being bad! Actually, it's the greatest, single piece of intelligence to come our way for years. That strip of film contains detailed photographs of the circuitry used in the Soviet's top-secret missiles. And that includes their *Scrag* as well as their multiple warheads. Do you realize what this means?"

Before I could open my mouth, he raced on.

"It means we'll have the Russians over the barrel during the next round of SALT talks. For the past few years our people in State have had to second guess the Russians on what they had or didn't have in their arsenal. But now we *know*. And there's only one way the Russians can get around this, and that's to scrap some of their most important rockets and start over again. Putting it another way, it means we can now bargain with them from a position of strength which was something we simply couldn't do before."

I had an uncontrollable urge to grin, but I fought the impulse down.

"In that case, sir," I asked. "What is disturbing you?"

He slapped his hand down on my report. "This, N3! Getting your hands on that strip of film after Salobin died was absolutely sheer brillance on your part, but it just as easily could have gone the other way. If that girl's bullet had killed Salobin outright, the mission would have been torpedoed right then and there. Everything would have gone down the drain."

He was right, of course, and I knew it all too well.

"AXE wouldn't be what it is today without you, Nick," he said almost gently. "You know that."

I thanked him, got up.

"Nick," he said when I got to the door.

"Yes?"

"This Maya." He paused. "I wish she would have been on our side."

I nodded. "So do I, sir."

It was almost dusk when I left the building. I was about to hop a cab to my hotel, but decided to walk. As I headed south the sky behind the Washington Monument took on a soft, violet hue. It reminded me of Maya's eyes. It reminded me of a lot of other things as well.

THRILLERS

0352	Star	
397012	Georges Arnaud **THE WAGES OF FEAR**	50p
396474	Paul Boncarrere **ULTIMATUM**	75p
396962	William F. Buckley Jr. **SAVING THE QUEEN**	60p*
396059	Richard Butler **WHERE ALL THE GIRLS ARE SWEETER**	60p
398736	Eric Corder **THE BITE**	60p*
300523	Henry Denker **A PLACE FOR THE MIGHTY**	75p*
398582	Burt Hirschfeld **'FATHER PIG!'**	60p*
396253	Tony Kenrick **THE SEVEN DAY SOLDIERS**	60p
396679	David Lippincott **TREMOR VIOLET**	75p
396849	Hugh C. McDonald **THE HOUR OF THE BLUE FOX**	60p
395982	Graham Masterton **PLAGUE**	75p
396911	**FIREFLASH 5**	60p
395818	Michael Maguire **SCRATCHPROOF**	70p
397853	**SLAUGHTER HORSE**	70p

CRIME

0352	Star			
396261	Christopher Robbins **ASSASSIN**	(NF)	(illus)	70p
398639	Donald Rumbelow **THE COMPLETE JACK THE RIPPER**	(NF)	(illus)	60p

†For sale in Britain and Ireland only.
*Not for sale in Canada.

†For sale in Britain and Ireland only.
*Not for sale in Canada.

GENERAL FICTION

0352 Star

396423	Mary Ann Ashe **RING OF ROSES**	60p
396938	Andre P. Brink **LOOKING ON DARKNESS**	95p
39613X	William Burroughs **DEAD FINGERS TALK**	75p
398663	Jackie Collins **THE WORLD IS FULL OF DIVORCED WOMEN**	50p
398752	**THE WORLD IS FULL OF MARRIED MEN**	50p
300671	Eric Corder **HELLBOTTOM**	75p*
300086	**THE LONG TATTOO**	40p*
398515	**RUNNING DOGS**	60p*
396113	Robertson Davies **FIFTH BUSINESS**	95p
396857	Terry Fisher **IF YOU'VE GOT THE MONEY**	70p
39840X	Knight Isaacson **THE STORE**	60p
396105	Gavin Lambert **IN THE NIGHT ALL CATS ARE GREY**	75p
396334	**THE SLIDE AREA**	75p
398299	Robin Maugham **THE SIGN**	55p*
397594	Clayton Moore **END OF RECKONING**	60p*
397608	**141 TERRACE DRIVE**	60p*
397543	**RIVER FALLS**	60p*
397667	**SECRET FIRE**	60p*
397659	**THE CORRUPTERS**	60p*
397551	**WESLEY SHERIDAN**	60p*
300809	Molly Parkin **LOVE ALL**	50p
397179	**UP TIGHT**	60p
396946	Judith Rossner **TO THE PRECIPICE**	85p*

†For sale in Britain and Ireland only.
*Not for sale in Canada.

GENERAL FICTION

Alan Sillitoe
397144	THE FLAME OF LIFE	70p
398892	THE GENERAL	50p
300965	THE LONELINESS OF THE LONG DISTANCE RUNNER	50p
300949	MEN, WOMEN AND CHILDREN	50p
398809	THE RAGMAN'S DAUGHTER	50p
300981	SATURDAY NIGHT AND SUNDAY MORNING	50p

Hubert Selby Jr.
| 396415 | THE ROOM | 75p |

Ernest Tidyman
| 398884 | STARSTRUCK | 60p* |

0426   Tandem

Gerty Agoston
| 162560 | MY BED IS NOT FOR SLEEPING | 50p* |

Nigel Balchin
175824	THE BORGIA TESTAMENT	60p
175905	THE SMALL BACK ROOM	60p
176030	MINE OWN EXECUTIONER	60p
176111	A SORT OF TRAITORS	60p

Bill Bavin
| 180593 | THE DESTRUCTIVE VICE | 75p |

Catherine Cookson
163796	THE GARMENT	60p
163524	HANNAH MASSEY	60p
163605	SLINKY JANE	60p

Jean Francis
| 162803 | COMING AGAIN | 45p* |

John Goulet
| 182278 | THE HUMAN APE | 75p* |

Brian Hayles
| 165209 | SPRING AT BROOKFIELD | 50p |

Harrison James
| 172167 | ABDUCTION | 50p* |

Julie Lawrence
| 151577 | BLONDES DON'T HAVE ALL THE FUN! | 50p* |

Keith Miles
| 16539X | AMBRIDGE SUMMER | 50p |

Betty Smith
178815	JOY IN THE MORNING	70p*
179455	MAGGIE: NOW	75p*
178734	TOMORROW WILL BE BETTER	70p*

†For sale in Britain and Ireland only.   *Not for sale in Canada.

Wyndham Books are obtainable from many booksellers and newsagents. If you have any difficulty please send purchase price plus postage on the scale below to:

Wyndham Cash Sales,
P.O. Box 11,
Falmouth,
Cornwall

OR

Star Book Service,
G.P.O. Box 29,
Douglas,
Isle of Man,
British Isles

While every effort is made to keep prices low, it is sometimes necessary to increase prices at short notice. Wyndham Books reserve the right to show new retail prices on covers which may differ from those advertised in the text or elsewhere.

Postage and Packing Rate
U.K.
One book 22p plus 10p per copy for each additional book ordered to a maximum charge of 82p.

B.F.P.O. and Eire
One book 22p plus 10p per copy for the next 6 books and thereafter 4p per book. Overseas 30p for the first book and 10p per copy for each additional book.